~~

About the Cover

The Filled Julia Set is a variation on the Mandelbrot Set, another mathematical figure. The difference between the two is swapping how the two variables are handled in the equation $f(x) = z^2 + c$, also starting iterations at any given complex number in the unit circle. The particular starting value for this cover is -0.8 + i0.156.

Similar to the rendition on the cover, my writing style lacks the fine descriptions and details you may find in other books and stories (or other Filled Julia Sets or Mandelbrot Sets) so that you may imagine the fine details of the following stories for yourself and experience the stories in your own unique way.

Please Enjoy.

ISBN 978-1-0878-7605-4

51499

9 781087 876054

~~

Discords of The Mind Vol. 2

A Collection of Short Stories

By BC. Neon

~~

Table Of Contents

~~

Across The Moonlit Desert

"I think you'll do best at the school of magic, Ilus," the king says. Something isn't right.

"I beg to differ, my lord," I reply, "My combat skills are supreme."

"But you are also from the mainland; a peasant," he tells me.

The deep ring of a bell erases the world around me, and a crack of steel brings me to a desert; white sands and single, striking moon condescending on me, for it knows I'll never conquer it. Something isn't right.

"Ilus stupid Everaurd," I hear a familiar voice, "I've come to finally collect your soul."

"I've died, haven't I?" I ask my old friend.

"Yes, and I hope I get to drag you to the deepest rings of hell," he replies. I look behind me to see the great grim reaper; the old one; the soul collector.

He slams his staff with five arms into the ground, breaking the very earth beneath him; chains fly out from the arms, chasing for my life and limb, but I know the magic of this world and I reject them.

An invisible shield deflects the chains away, and they slowly burn away into scale. "Now you've done it Ilus!" he shouts as the arms fall away and a single grim blade grows from the head of the staff. "Now I've come to collect your soul once and for all!"

He swings the blade to and fro, but I dodge each attack by the hairs on my head. One swing after another, unable to land a single slice. As I bide my time, I think of a teleportation spell that's viable in this world.

Suddenly, it comes to me; I force nature to bend to my will as the greatest magician who has ever lived in all of time and the world around me shifts about. I look around to see where I've landed and I see the reaper a long ways walk.

"Ilus!" he shrieks into the night, calling upon the forces of his darkness. Hellhounds begin to claw their way from the sands of this moonlit desert, snarling and thrashing their way to the surface. I cast the spell once more with more concentration and I hear with pure fury before I shift, "Find him!"

I cast and carve the circles and spells into the striking white sand, and as I finish, I glare back up at the moon who always watches. The moon represents God and the sun as mortals, or the current lack thereof from what I've read.

I begin to meditate and the sands refine themselves into my familiar weapon of choice: my chain-sword, the *harbringer*. I reach out and rest my hand on the weapon and pull it from the air, blade reaching and swirling all around form this earth.

I hear the hounds in the distance, snarling and snatching, chasing me as far as they can, but they are mindless creatures with a single goal in mind.

I form another weapon from the desert and ready myself for their attack. They come, and I slice them down, the creatures from hell, one after another. Their flesh tears and burns away into the nothingness they came from.

I see farther into the horizon and see him chasing me, with a new weapon in hand, and I disappear.

I've finally found it: the house of the gods; its form in this world is quaint, modest. A simple, double-heighted house sitting in front of an enormous sand dune. I walk up to the door, and I hear another familiar voice from inside.

"Come in, Ilus," Andega, the very embodiment of time, tells me. I walk through the creaking door and reveal an empty home, void of all amenities give a single chair that I find him sitting in. "Welcome, Ilus," he says.

"Hello," I greet him.

"You've done it," he says, standing and walking to an overgrown shrub, stroking it's forbidden branches of time and space, "We chased you till the end of time itself, and now it's time for us to go."

"Where to go, exactly?" I ask.

"All of us," he tells me, "You're the last soul."

I hear the footsteps closing in, that of the great reaper. "Don't worry," Andega tells me, "I've called him off. I'll escort you to the higher courts."

The door opens and I see an old, beaten reaper who has spent all of time chasing something he could not catch. Andega leaves the shrub and escorts me out the door, into the great beyond. I look back at the shrub to find it falling away into nothingness, starting at the roots.

"I've reviewed all of your work, Andega," the man in the highest chair says, "And you're a failure.

"And this thing you've allowed in our realms; disgusting."

"I'll have you know-" I attempt to correct them.

He snarks back at me, "You'll have me know what, Ilus? That you're the greatest magician of all time?"

"Yes!" I cry out. My voice echoes in the great white and golden halls.

"Then I'll take it from you," he replies, reaching his hand out to pull at my soul strings, but my protections resist his pull, rejecting him even. He pulls back, visibly angry.

"I'm afraid he is, Homm, that he is indeed a great magician," Andega tells him, "Even greater than I was."

The other members of this higher court murmur amongst themselves, until one of them speaks out, "I shall bring my champion to challenge him!" The one raises his hand and summons a man from nothingness. I stare down this opponent of mine, shaven head and a cloth covering his legs.

"You are a champion?" I ask him.

I look about his surroundings, trying to realize where he is. "I suppose I am, Ilus. I was, too, the greatest sorcerer of my world; a different world where you never existed."

"Regardless, I am the greatest magician of dimension 3 as I've been told it was called." the man with the body carved from stone begins to approach me. He comes just shy of me and sits down on the ground. And I too, sit down with him and I hear them snap their fingers.

I find him in the mindscape and we converse about the things of magic until there is none more to discuss. He rises in the presence of the judges and confesses, "I'm no match for him." as he speaks, he is summoned away.

"Cast him in ring 8!" one of the judges cry out.

Another starts waving his arm in the sky, "Might as well send him to ring 9 if we do that!"

The judge hushes their chatter, "Andega! You will be dealt with later." the Judge tries again with more intent to dispel my curses and spells I have carved into my body and soul, but it's to no avail and burns his hands. "And this monstrosity will be cast down to the deepest pit of hell!"

Another grim reaper wraps his chains around my impenetrable protections and begins pulling me through the dimensions.

I fall through the infinite sea of eternal creation, down further than books could describe. Suddenly, I find myself face to face with the three-faced man, some describe him as the devil; legend has told me that he rules the underworld and resides in the deepest level of this hell, 11 dimensions down.

"Oh, the gods have sent me a gift," his middle face says, "Who might you be?"

I stand to my feet and brush off my clothes, "I am Ilus Everaurd, greatest magician in all of creation-"

His left two heads begin to cackle, whilst his rightmost head begins to speak, "In all of creation, you say?"

I cast my most advanced spell to bind him, "Hado 999: God Trap!" a magical cuff wraps around his neck and a chain sprouts down to my fingertips.

The center face speaks again, "This is indeed impressive, something like this could cause me an issue." The other two faces still continue to cackle. He reaches to crush the cuff that binds him, but I've used up the rest of my magic. "Now, let me think this through before we do anything rash-"

The rightmost head speaks, "What could possibly benefit us from this trap?"

"He wishes to absorb the magic of this world-" the leftmost tells the other two.

"And this spell will slowly drain the magic from us into his body-"

The rightmost cuts him off, "And we want to see what will happen?"

The left two agree in unison. "So let us see this through," he lowers his hand. Suddenly his magic begins to flow through the chain and into my familiar.

It's cold and dark magic, the very opposite of what evolved from my timeline. Truly the dark magic the king tried so hard to banish from my world.

I look out a window to see the creatures of hell swirling around the sky and pacing out the door; leviathans, hellhounds, the sort. The leviathan outside this very window is gigantic, larger than I ever could've begun to imagine, different than in the books I've read about the deep.

"Tell me your name, monster," I command.

"Now don't get cocky, Ilus," he replies, "I can break this spell at any moment I please, but call me Zaefus, for now."

"Zaefus, can you command the leviathans?"

"We are the ruler of all 11 dimensions below 0," all three of his head laughs, "Of course we can."

I pull on the chain of my new pet: the three-faced man. I feel the dark magic flowing into me through the chain that links us two. We walk out of this dark temple and into the hellscape. I see lost souls burning in the deep sulfur and monsters flying on high with floating temples to pagan gods interspersed throughout the spaces.

I reach my hand out into the painful air at a leviathan, recalling in the books their immense resilience, trying to summon it.

"What are you doing?" one of his faces snarks.

"I'm summoning a vessel to travel through-"

"Do you really think you could control one of them?"

"Yes-" I reach out and cast a spell to bring it here. It slowly veers and smashes into a floating citylet.

"Oh, so we see."

It starts flying down toward us and crashes at my feet. I walk along and pull the dark lord with me. "What do you plan to do with this creature?"

"You shall see, won't you."

I summon a *harbringer* from the armor of the leviathan and stand upon its head.

As the dimensions break open time after time, we make our way up into the heavens. I see the vast scapes below of suffering of every kind. The break in time and space sounds like a deep bell, rung deep within my bones.

I counted thirteen as the wind blows through my hair. "How far do you intend on going?" he asks. I look to see my world, advanced beyond my wildest dreams.

"All of it, All of creation!" the leviathan begins to change as we pass through another portal. The bell rings again, painfully throughout my head. The leviathan changes again, I feel it's flesh transform instantaneously as we pass into the new dimension. I see the moonlit desert that began this journey.

"Beware Ilus, you're doing what's never been done," one of his faces speaks to me, and his right face interrupts, "It hasn't been done because no one has survived it."

We go through another and another, nothing stopping me, but I feel that each jump requires more magic than the last and not even the leviathan is surviving. The beast is shrinking beneath my feet and changing in the blink of an eye to something new.

"I intend to be the greatest in all of creation!" I shout against the wind.

Finally, I count twenty some odd worlds, and the leviathan falls out of the sky as a worm beneath my feet. I tumble around the fertile soil that now surrounds us. I look up to see the three-faced man walking down an invisible staircase. As I focus my eyes, I see the gods of the heavens beyond the books I read in Andega's library.

Some of them gasp in horror.

"Hark! Who goes there!?" I hear someone ask. I get up to my feet and brush away the mossy soil I'm covered in. They all look like vagabonds in white gowns roaming the forest, but I feel their immense magical strength.

"My name is Ilus *bragging* Everaurd," I declare. They murmur amongst themselves in some celestial language. *I've heard of him*, one says. *Who is that?* Another goes on.

An elderly man walks out of the circle around me. "I've heard of you, a mortal from the lowest reach of creation, he who tries to create," he says, "He who challenges God."

"So you've heard very little about me," I reply, readying a spell to break through another world.

The three-faced man looks unsettled as I look back at him, but ready nonetheless. "Are you ready?"

The left face cackles, "You don't know what lies beyond this barrier, Ilus." I thrust my hand towards that elderly man who speaks against me, breaking through space and time with the dark magic I've leeched off the three-faced man.

I push my fingers, nearly breaking them, as I feel the other side. Purple-colored lightning crackles from my hand, burning little marks all around, even singeing the hairs on arm through my many layers of protection cursed into my soul. I push along until the tear begins to consume my arm, then I force my body through it. And what I see is magnificent, more than anything else I've seen.

I see a single man, smooth and defined like a stone sculpture wrapped in white cloth sitting on a stool. The universe surrounds him in it's rawest form. He looks upon me and stands to his feet as I continue to walk towards him. I feel some resistance from my prisoner and I yanked him through with an exciting crack of lightning. I look back as he falls to the ground. He's sweating like a coward. The god before me look upon me in silence.

"I-" try to introduce myself.

"You disgust me Zaefus," the white man commands, "Begone."

He raises two fingers up and the three-faced man disintegrated, skin then bones to dust.

I clear my throat, readying a spell. "Do you think you can defeat me, Ilus Everaurd?

"You claim to be the greatest magician in all of creation and wish to challenge God."

"Yes-" he interrupts me again, his voice like an unstoppable wall of stone, grinding everything to dust.

"I stand upon the pinnacle of *all* creation and even I am not God," he speaks, "How pious."

"I am-"

"You are nothing, Ilus. I was born an only child of this universe and I created; you are the dirt beneath my feet," he raises his two fingers and he dispels all of the magic in me; all my curses and enchantments I've burned into myself and my soul throughout all my life- all gone.

I feel bare, like a child without clothes. I look down at my hands, now clear and bare. "What-what did you do to me."

"So you survived?" he continues, "How interesting. No wonder Homm could not sentence you to death.

"Now, *begone.*" I feel nothing as I return from whence I came.

August 30, 2132

Sequel to December 19, 2099

"What are you doing?" My partner walks in, looking at me hunched over on the computer. I look up to see him, holding the two coffees for both of us.

"You know me," I tell her, grabbing my beverage, "looking at old files for something new to learn."

"I know from experience," she says to me, "You'll learn what you need to know out in the field, not on a computer."

"I'm obsessed with being the best, you know that." I take a sip on the iced drink, savoring it as I swallow.

"What are you even looking at?"

I scroll up to the top of the file. "It's a closed homicide file; of-," I pause, "One Detective Jameson."

"What year was that?" she asks, bending down to look for herself.

"Uh, '23," I take another sip, "It's kinda sketchy; the guy gets killed, his partner gets sent straight to high security without trial under, uh, EC-113."

"That's definitely fishy, but it wouldn't be the first time," She stands back up, blowing on her hot coffee, "There's a lot of crooked cops covering things up."

"Well, he did lie on a federal classification exam, so who knows."

"Let's go and do some actual work, you *rookie*." she messes up my hair and pulls me up from my chair, "There's some young man who needs paperwork done, *and* your the man to do it."

We walk through the door and enter the bustling of midnight workers running around doing all the last-minute work before the workers come in in the morning.

"Who's in now?" my partner asks aloud.

"A regular- Anglé Altor."

"Him again?" I try to look past the corner to see the white room. I rush to get behind the glass and grab the microphone.

"An, what did we discuss?" I ask him as a cop cuffs him to the table.

"Entertainment- I should be in entertainment-"

"Yes!" I affirm, "What did you do now?"

The other officers behind me start laughing, "Go ahead and tell him, An!"

"I'm not-" he's interrupted by laughing.

"You'll get a kick out of this," my partner tells me, handing me the report. I look it over and find the crime: stealing a bad magazine from his regular convenience store.

"Seriously, An?!" I say into the microphone. He turns tomato red, "What happened to candy bars and soda?"

"I mean- what do you want from me?" he retorts.

"I want you to get a job!" I shout at him, "You can make things disappear in your hands, for crying out loud!"

"Ugh," I lightly bang my head on the wall, "How long is he going to be here?"

"A couple of hours until the business owner calls and lets him loose," he breaks down laughing again, "Kids these days."

"Just get me the papers so I can fill them out," I say, turning off the microphone and walking back out. My partner follows me out.

"On second thought, I'll have Jefferson doing the papers this time, we have to go out for something. Nevermind the paperwork."

She herds me to the front of the office and we make it outside to the warm, midnight summer air blowing everything about. We make out way to our vehicle. We get in and I turn the key, starting the old hydrogen engine. These cars are on their deathbed, but the city won't replace all of them at once; the state starving us for funds.

"Where to?" I ask.

"*We* just got assigned to a new case-" the car phone starts ringing and we look at each other. She smiles and I raise my brow; she insists with her hand that I pick it up.

The car phone starts talking, "Detective Olsen?"

"Yes, Sargent?" I reply

"Is your partner with you?" he asks, with some rustling of paper on the other end of the phone.

"Yes, Sargent."

"Good, I'm assigning you two to a homicide on the other side of town, figured it'll get your feet a little wet." I look at my partner with a mixture of emotions.

"Yessir, we're already on our way," I tell him.

"Good, I like your enthusiasm," he says, "9142 cricket." Kekik mouths along with Sargent. He promptly hangs up the phone.

"*Chronosight*," she reminds me with her jazzy fingers.

The car kicks into gear and we start moving. Traffic on this side of the city is usually pretty busy all day round, accidents left and right of the ghetto. We get through the downtown border to find this 'Cricket' street, and it doesn't take long. We arrive to see a home swarming with officers and we pull up.

"Bring us up to speed," My partner demands from one of the people standing around.

"Oh, it's you," the guy says as he turns around, signaling to some others that there's finally a detective on the scene. He looks back and just raises his hands up, "What? You don't know what I'm going to say?"

"I'd rather not exhaust myself on you," she replies, pulling out a notepad, "What do you know?"

"Family of 3, breaking and entering, oldest son cooked him alive; he's waiting over in the car."

"Cooked how?" she asks, marching up to the home to look inside.

"Electrocution!" he shouts to her, "The smell-"

"Aw!" Kekik yells out in disgust, "What died in here?" I rush behind her, getting a whiff of the horrible smell.

"Kekik, I think that's a little insensitive," I tell her.

"What, it's the bad guy that died," she says, writing in her notepad. I wave my hand to get the bad air away from me. "What do you see?"

I look around, see the broken door, count the items knocked over on the counter, and finally, the perpetrator burned to a crisp in the corner. "A see a fairly common killed man, what do you see?"

She turns and I see her eyes dilated to black, "I see excessive force, that he struggled and tried to escape." her eyes return to normal and she rubs her head. She starts writing everything down, furiously on the notepad while walking back outside, presumably to escape the smell.

We make it outside and some masked cleanup people go in behind us. "What'd you see this time, Kekik?" he asks.

"Excessive force; thug tried to escape, but the son wouldn't let him and killed him," she replies, walking straight passed him to the kid being held in the car. She points to the kid and another officer rolls down the window. She's walking so fast, I can barely keep up, but she stops at the car, and I'm not too far behind.

I look inside the car to see the kid in cuffs and a C-dampener clamped around his neck, shining green light everywhere. "So, kid," she says.

"So what?" he replies, not casting his gaze away from the car seat in front of him.

"You know what," she leans over into the window, "You just killed a man-"

"It was in self-defense."

"You can't hide anything from me," she persists, "Did he try to escape?"

"No, he- he attacked me-"

"I possess the ability to see 12 hours in the past," she explains, "*Did he try to escape?*" the kid starts to shake and tear up.

"Yes," he finally confesses, "He was violent, though and I didn't realize he was try- I just-" he stops mid-sentence and Kekik starts writing down his confessions.

She turns to me, "We have all we need now." I look over to the house to see the body bag being ushered out by the men in white suits.

I go back to that closed case for one detective Jameson, something really doesn't seem right; 'always trust your gut,' I was told during training, and my gut doesn't like the way it ended. There has to be more. I could ask Sargent about it, he probably knew the guy.

I stand up from my desk and make my way through the office, avoiding all the other officers running around. My partner is standing outside of his door. If I recall, she's not allowed into his office for confidentiality reasons, as she can see everything within the past 12 hours.

"What are you waiting for?" I ask her.

"Just wanted to ask him about our next assignment, it's been nothing but paperwork since last time."

I peer through his blinds, looking at him on the phone. "Well, maybe it's just a slow season for crime."

"Please-" she snorts, "There's never a slow day in this city."

The door opens suddenly and his head pokes right out, "What are you two waiting for?"

I signal to my partner. "Just wondering when you're going to send us out again." she steps forward, but Sargent stops her.

"You're not to step over this threshold, detective," he barks, "there hasn't been a crime needing your caliber of ability.

"Now, you," he grabs me, pulling me into his office, "What do you need?"

"I was actually going to ask you about an old case," I tell him, "For research?"

"Which one?" he sits down in his chair. I look at his family photo; his kid looks like a cancer patient without any hair, his eyes sunken in. Sargent doesn't talk about him at all.

"Detective Jameson's homicide-"

"Aw, hell," he exclaims, "What do you want to know about that?"

I sit down in the other chair. "I don't know, I wanted some insight; on paper, it seems fishy, detective Zeemo-"

"Carter Zeemo was a very dirty cop and guilty beyond doubt," he explains, "The state sought to, in their infinite wisdom, send him to high security immediately because he was dangerous."

"What was his classification?"

"He could stop nerve impulses by touch," He leans back in his chair, "*which*, he lied about on a federal classification exam!

"Do everyone a favor, and leave that case the way it is: *closed.*"

"Yessir," I say, standing back up and heading for the door, "How's the kid?"

"He's better, he's been sick for a while, but he's finally getting better. Thank you."

I see myself out of his office and meet up with my partner. We go to the foyer for the coffee machine and I start on a batch. "What'd he say?" she asks, pouring herself a mug.

"I want to reopen the case," I tell her, pouring myself some of the coffee, "He thought otherwise."

"So what are you going to do? You can't reopen without his permission."

"I'm going to investigate a little more in my free time." I quickly drink the last of the hot drink. "Any more paperwork I need to do?"

"I'll have other people on it," she tells me, drinking the rest of her coffee too, "Where to, detective?"

"Let's go to the evidence vault, whadya' you say?"

She nods and we walk outside, warm air blowing beneath us as we walk. I look up at the moon, it's about halfway tonight. We get to the car and I notice a new dent in the roof; one of the other officers must've gotten a rock thrown at him. Either way, we get into the vehicle and go on our way.

"So, do you know when all the red lights are going to hit?" I jokingly ask, turning out of the parking lot.

"I have to *want* to see the red lights, y'know." I swerve the car to avoid an oncoming vehicle that just ran the apposing red light, but that's not my job.

The evidence vault is state run in the center of the city. It contains all evidence for every case for the past 10 years, before being sent off to a larger vault every fall. Big building; dark blue and silver pillars running up the sides.

I make the right turn, another police car very narrowly missing me making his right turn, into the lot and make our way through the convoluted parking situation.

"There's a spot on the other side," she lets me know.

"Chronosight?" I ask.

"No, just perception." I turn around and find that spot she was talking about and we make our way into the building. The inside is just as modern architecture as the outside: white concrete and silver pillars. We flash our badges to get past the guards by the front and get to the desk.

"Good evening, officers," the desk lady greets us, "How can I help you today?"

"I'd like to see some archived evidence from a case in '23," I tell her.

"Case ID?" she asks, typing on the desk computer.

I give her the case number and all the relative information, "and it's a state case."

"Alright, give me one moment," she says to me, typing vigorously on the keyboard, "Got it; what's the reason for accessing the evidence?"

"I'm conducting an, uh, *unofficial* investigation to reopen that particular case."

"Alright, follow me," she stands up, grabbing a small printout and a large ring of keys in hand, "Can I see both your badges?"

"Yes, of course," I signal to my partner and we hand them over to the lady. She looks them over and hands them back.

"What's your manifestation?" she asks Kekik.

"I can focus on events either up to 12 hours in the past or 3 seconds in the future," she explains.

"Fascinating," she replies, "I bet that comes in handy. Follow me, *detectives.*"

She leads us to a large vault door, opening with an analog set of three keys. The two steel doors swing open with a gust of wind in the face and we enter to another set of door with three more keys. The final vault doors enter into a maze of black evidence lockers 10 feet tall.

"Follow me, it's easy to get lost in here," she reminds us, grabbing and pulling along a steel step ladder. Twisting and turning down these hallways, we finally stop. She climbs up the ladder and unlocks the locker, pulling out a box and walking back down.

"Here we go, detectives," she says, setting the box on one of the steps. I look around in the box; the final report, a gun, a phone, several bullets and the like.

I pick up the phone, turning on the archaic flip-phone from the early 2000s. The animation plays and the *home* screen plays in. I note the last few numbers called on the device, sure that one of them contains what I need. I recognize Sargent's number somewhere down the list, along with some other names.

"Thank you, I have what I need," I tell the lady, turning off the phone and setting it back in the box.

I stamp the very last of the paperwork, right before the door bursts open revealing an angry Sargent. "My office, now!" he barks. I stand up and march along behind him across the workplace. I step beyond the threshold of his office and the door slams behind me.

"What the hell, Walk? He shouts, "I got word that you went to the state's evidence vault, looking at Jameson's evidence."

"I-"

"Shut it! I told you, *specifically*, to leave this case alone," he pinches his fingers together.

"I intend on reopening this case-"

"I won't let you," he barks.

"Then I'll have the state reopen it for me!" I shout back at him, "There's something more-"

"There's *always* something more, dimwit. But you *need* to learn when to and not to dig something up," he slams on his desk, "This is when not to."

"No," I whisper.

"What was that?" he snarks.

"No," I speak up, "I was told to always trust my gut, and I'm trusting it."

"And you'll regret it just like Jameson," he leans back, putting his hand over his face, "Get out of my office."

I turn tail and go back to my office. I wiggle the mouse and turn the screen back on. I take out the note I made with the phone numbers. I type in the most recent one into our database, pulling up someone who was jailed in '24; apparently a whistle blower that was able to escape arrest for an entire year after being associated with the case.

My door opens and my partner greets me. "Let's go investigate," we say in unison.

"You just love that," I tell her.

"If you can, why not. Let's go; where to?"

"Jailhouse right outside the city." We start walking out to the car, but Kekik grabs me and pulls me along to another vehicle.

"What-"

"Trust me," she says, going inside the driver's seat. As soon as I get in the passenger, we drive off into the night. "So what did Sargent say to you?"

"He got word that we went to the vault, and he wasn't happy; said he's not going to let me reopen." she swerves the car to right, missing an oncoming accident. "Geez."

"Sounds like you're in a pickle," she replies, "Do you know how to appeal to the state directly? Because I have a state connection."

"Well, let's go see this person at the prison first." We get to the edge of the city, coming up to the border of the next one over where the prison is located.

The prison is just a set of concrete walls, big tower in the middle. We pulls up and make our way to the entrance. We flash our badges and march right on in.

"Good evening," the desk man greets us, flashing our badges, "What can we do for you, detectives?"

"We need to see Ben Stick?" I ask of him.

"He's in the medical ward, he can't receive visitors."

"We're conducting an investigation and need to see him immediately-"

"He's being treated for a stab wound, another prisoner just shived him *literally* 5 minutes ago-"

"We *need* to see him, that's an order," Kekik demands. The desk man shrugs his shoulders and signals to one of the men at the door to lead us to him. The door beeps and creaks open.

He leads us all the way down a hall before opening the door, and we're greeted with an empty room give a single man suffering on a bed. "That's the guy you're looking for," the man says, closing the door.

"Can you wait outside, officer?" Kekik asks the man. He shrugs and walks outside.

"Aw, hell," he turns to us, "I didn't say *anything!* I swear, he just-"

Kekik starts talking in unison with the man, "Was waiting for my food-"

"What the?"

"I'm detective Walker, and this is detective Kekik," I introduce ourselves, "I'm here to ask you about the death of detective Jameson."

"No," he turns his head, "Nope, nada, nothing from me, I'm not saying anything about that." he turns and holds his stomach.

"You need-"

"*Legally speaking*," he turns my way, "I can keep my mouth shut."

"My associate-"

"What is this? Good cop-bad cop?" he snarks, "You're not getting anything from me." My partner motions to me to leave. She knocks on the door and the guard waiting outside opens up.

"Do you mind if we tour the facility?" she asks. He nods and we walk back into the hallway. Kekik starts leading the way through the door and turns of the prison, eventually leading us to the perfectly empty mess hall.

"What do you see?" I ask her as she starts wandering around the hall, looking and listening for something. She follows a path from the table to the serving area, looking underneath one of the tables before following her chronosight across the hall.

"Hey, what's she doin'?" the guard asks.

"She has a set of *skills*, you could say," I tell him, leaning on the wall.

"*Naw*," he laughs, "She a 25?"

"She's not very fond of that term." she walks up to one of the phones, pulls out her notepad as I rush over to her as she seems to be listening very carefully at something. I peer over her shoulder to see what she's writing: dialogue and a phone number. Her eyes return to normal and she hands me the notepad.

"This is hot stuff," I read it over, "Who is it though?"

"They used a voice synth," she tells me, "But I have a hunch."

Kekik and I arrive at the state's investigation bureau, from our drive from our office. Today's a day off for both of us, so we took her personal vehicle down south to the state's jurisdiction.

We walk up to the 2-inch bullet-resistant glass. "How can you be helped today?" the person on the other side says to us. I look up to see cameras on every corner of the wall, looking, searching. It's even worse than in the city.

"I'd like to see Walter Gress," Kekik tells the person, flashing her badge.

"What for?" the person snarks, typing on the computer.

"I need to talk with him about getting a search warrant against my superior." the lady raises her eyebrow, stopping her typing.

"What's your classification?" she goes back on the computer.

"chronosight, class 4," she puts her classification card on the window. The lady keeps typing after a long awkward pause of conversation. She waves her hand and we walk to the guard by the detector and the conveyor belt. We empty ourselves into a box and walk through the advanced detector.

Kekik walks through, but is stopped and the guard puts a chromosome suppressor around her neck, and a powerful one too. Her head twitches as it activates and she's herded through the detector.

"We'll keep all necessary items here until you're done," the man says. He puts a lid on the boxes and scans them, placing them to the side. I roll my eyes and another guard leads us through some doors

"Kekik!" a man shouts with a certain twang in his voice, "Holy ho! What can I do 'fer you?"

"Walter!" she greets him. He waves the guard away and starts leading us himself. He opens a door and we go into a small office without any windows, white walls and a blue carpet.

"I need a favor," she lead forward to his ear, whispering, "I need a warrant and your most powerful chronoseeing officer."

"Holy ho, Kekik, I git you," he replies. He starts to whimsically typing on the keyboard, bobbing back and forth in a happy jig. "What's ther' name, 'hon?"

She leans over and whispers Sargent's name in his ear, saying she needs someone to force entry into his office and someone to trace back everything he's done for as far back as possible.

He smashes a key and something starts printing out from beside him. "Done! Her be finis' by morrow's end."

"Don't we need a judge?" I ask my partner.

"We have a small network," she explains in a low voice, "there's a lot of crooks in this business; he has connections with a judge and a few others."

"Kekik, that's illegal," I remind her.

"So is being a crook."

"Lemma see y'out," the man stands up, and starts leading us out. The guard sees us as we walk out and rushes to pull us along. They wave goodbye as we pass through the doorway to the foyer.

We get to the detector and Kekik says, "Get this damn thing off me!" she lifts her head and the guard puts in the key and unlocks it, dimming the green light.

I take the step beyond the detector, and suddenly, the ground jumps up, shaking everything. I catch my feet, and the ground jumps again with an enormous crack breaking up the front wall. Kekik shoves the guard to open her box, followed by another jump.

The front wall shatters and falls down, Kekik jumps into action, brandishing her gun, with some other guards following. Smoke starts filling all around in the building. Some of the light from the outside fills out the smoke, showing a silhouette of the perpetrator standing by the fallen concrete.

The ground jumps again and the smoke reverberates with it, seeing the wave propagate out. Some more pieces of the concrete fall to the ground. I look over to my partner whose eyes are wide and chronoseeing into the future.

"Kekik! What do you see?" I shout, digging through the box to get my gun, right before the ground really jumps and part of the ceiling collapse by the front of the building, letting more light through the thick smoke.

She fires a few delicate shots, but the figure remains standing. Some of the other guards fire their weapons, but nothing seems to hit him. Again, the ground jumps and the tiles crack beneath me, shearing my feet apart.

Some guard with a long tail runs headfirst into the smoke, disappearing into it before being jettisoned out by another wave of seismic energy disturbing the structure even more. Kekik runs round about the cloud of smoke, but some chunks of building fall, obscuring her path.

The criminal screams out, rumbling the ground and breaking a piece from the ceiling directly above. I freeze in my steps, watching the cracks form, but Kekik tackles me, pushing both of us out of the way as it falls.

"I think there's two of 'em," she says, "One for the shakes, one for the smoke." she gets back on her feet and pulls me along. Sirens grow in the distance from the police station nearby.

Shot start firing from beyond the smoke, along with a few screams from the battle that's not in view. The smoke begins to clear, revealing extensive damages to the crumbling building and two individuals pinned to the ground.

My partner and I start walking towards them, stepping over and around the pieces of rubble. Her eyes grow wide, using her chronosight to see something. She goes off in her path, and I approach the police trying to wrangle the two with C-dampeners and handcuffs. The green lights grow brighter as they activate, putting an end to the terror.

One of the cops approaches me, "What the hell happened here?"

"They starts attacking, we're just inside and the wall came down-"

"Anyone dead?"

"No-"

"Targeted?" he keeps on.

"Can't tell." he rolls his eyes and walks off.

Kekik walks up to me, handing me her notepad. "My hunch is hunching, we need to head over there now and get hard evidence; he won't be expecting us."

"What about this-" I wave my hands at the whole mess.

"What about this?" she says, "We *need* to catch him."

"Wha-" one of the officers walks up to us, shaking his finger.

He marches up, "Where are you two going, you need to stay for a report."

Kekik pats down her body, looking for something before finally realizing her badge is still in the box. "I just- My badge-"

"Stay put!" he storms off. Kekik storms off in the other direction to presumably get her keys. She gets to the boxes and a guard stops her and they get into it.

I go over to the police car the two men are being pushed onto as they're being cuffed. I get to the officer standing there. "I'm detective Walker, I need to question these two."

"Badge?" he says. I pat down myself realizing mine is also in the box. He sees me coming up short as says, "Whatever, just get it on with."

I go past him to the struggling arrestee finally cuffed, but still causing a ruckus with a burly officer. He catches eye of me and stiffens up and starts whispering to the other, "Shit, we didn't kill him."

Kekik runs up, grabbing me by the arm and pulling me along back to the car with two boxes in hand and one of the guards walking after us. Last I see of the criminal is being hooked in the face. We get to the car and she tosses the boxes in through the window, sliding into the driver's seat.

"Hey!" the guy shouts, "Hey! You can't leave!" he reaches out for me, but I rush into the passenger. She starts backing up with the guy trying to stand in the way, smacking the back of the car. But he moves eventually and she slams on the accelerator, kicking dirt up at him.

Kekik steadily marches through the office, covered in dirt and dust, pushing past everyone in her path with me shortly behind. I look and see Sargent on the phone, looking up at us as we barrel through the office. He stands up and goes to the door, locking it, but Kekik kicks the door through, pausing traffic in the office and everything falling silent.

Sargent falls to the ground and I feel the air stiffen as Kekik uses her ability to the max, listening. Sargent pulls out a gun, but I pull out mine first and fire a shot through his arm spraying blood on the side of his desk.

Kekik looks down and picks him up, right before slugging him unconscious, letting him fall to the ground and cuffing him behind his back. "I'll read him his rights when he wakes up."

"Hunch was right?" I ask, grabbing the first aid kid.

"Very right; Walter will have that warrant ready by tomorrow and I'll have a chronoseer inspecting this place up and down."

"What do you hear?" I kneel down to address the bullet wound. She gets close to the chair and starts writing down in her notepad.

"He was calling a federal officer, saying we've dug too far. He needed us gone, so he sent someone to attack the SIB."

Sargent wakes from his knockout, groaning. I start reciting all the needed dialogue, picking him up and pulling him along to the white room. Everyone's frozen in place, silent as I haul him inside the white room.

"Jim-" I shout, "Jimmy! Come here!"

"What?!" he shouts back.

"Get the paperwork!"

Kekik walks out of the office, closing the door behind her. "Get the tape, everything!" she starts shouting commands, "That's a crime scene, everybody, get movin'!"

Everything starts up again, someone runs up, taping the door off limits. Another one of the officers walks up to Kekik, asking what's happening.

"Captured a crook," she tells him, "That's all; get back to work!"

Jimmy comes back with the paperwork, stumbling in to the back. "What the hell happened?" he asks me, starting to fill out the pages.

"He's a crook," I tell him, "treason and attempted murder, etcetera."

I open the front door to the office and I'm greeted with a hoard of state workers running the place, going through everything. I manage to make my way down to the Sargent's office, or should I say empty office as he was officially demoted yesterday.

I look over some shoulders and see the state's wondergirl, a class 7 chronosight meditating on the floor with some sort of EEG connected to a large machine printing out two continuous rolls of paper. Some sight to behold in person being around someone that high on the classification.

"What's she seeing?"

"When she, uh, gets like this," the man motions to the wondergirl, "She can go a couple months in the past."

I turn to look for Kekik, seeing if she's arrived this early in the morning. I think I see her brooding in her office, pacing back and forth. A very official looking man walks up, pushing past everyone to see the wondergirl. "You," he points at me, "Come with me."

We walk together to Kekik's office. He opens the door and I see Kekik pacing back and forth on the phone. "H-hey!" the man calls for her. She looks over and hangs up her phone, walking over to us. "You two busted thing a whole thing open, thought you might want an update," he says, closing the door behind himself, "He's been connected to over a *hundred* cases, and we're exposing a whole ring thanks to you guys, along with the evidence and testimony from Stick; we might even have to bring in the feds on this."

"That serious?" Kekik asks him, "Why wasn't this exposed already?"

"There's corruption on every level, it's possible it's been covered up," he responds, "If you'd like, I can add you two to the case."

Kekik motions to me. He opens the door back up and walks out back into the hustle. Kekik shuts the door and slides the lock too. "What now?" she asks.

"I don't know," I say, "This is the biggest break in our careers."

"Well, so far," she leans on her desk, "Anyways, the office is basically shut down until this is finished; we're not allowed to touch any of those cases either."

"Did you see the wondergirl over there?" I ask, motioning behind me.

"Yeah," she sounds angry, jealous almost, "I'm going to finish my phone call." She unlocks the door and leaves it open for me. I go back out to the bustle of state people running about inspecting the office top to bottom.

I get to my office, now empty of all physical files. I've never seen it so clean. The computer turns on and I start scrolling through the list of cases brought out of archive, listed 'reopened'. Homicide after homicide, drug trafficking, human trafficking, the list goes on.

And I see a ticket for Mr. Stick for unauthorized espionage. I open it up and look at it, reading the list of evidence that was submitted with it: a single notebook.

A knock on the door, and the head of this investigation walks in. "Have you decided?" he asks, looming in the doorway.

"Actually," I think about the precept of not being able to work otherwise until this investigation blows over, "I think I will."

"Good; we can use another man of your talents," he motions for me to follow him, so I shut down the program and start walking. I get through the door and immediately, a girl rushes by with a large stack of readouts from the wondergirl. "Those'll take weeks to analyze it, but it's all incriminating."

He rests his hand on my back and guides me to where he's going. He brings me to the empty office where the wondergirl is still at work on the ground with the machine she's connected to printing out another stack of papers.

"She'll go on for several more hours," he says, "She's one of our best resources for collecting evidence; y'know the feds don't even allow 25s in their arsenal due to some early legislation."

This office has been stripped to the walls, tape on everything that wasn't removed for fingerprints and an armored evidence truck being loaded with everything little dust mite that crawled beneath his feet. "What about a new sergeant?" I ask him.

"I'll have the city promote the senior officer in the building." he pulls me along away from the watching crowd towards the white room. "The things this room has seen," he pauses, "We'll be in contact with you and your partner." He pats my back and walks away. It's not even 7 in the morning yet, I haven't even had coffee.

The light a few cars down turns red, bringing traffic to a halt. The man leading the charge assigned us to go get information from an individual that scares even Kekik: Carter Zeemo. We're making the trek to the state's high security prison up north. I've never been, but I've been told it sticks out like a skyscraper in the suburbs.

The light goes green and we start going once more, trying to get on the interstate. "You seem tense, Kekik," I say, getting into the lane.

"I've read the guy's file, it's a little disturbing," she replies, pulling out her phone to pass the time for the 40 minute drive.

"Brief me," I ask her, "I was busy when they gave us access to the file."

She tells me that he kept the facade of being a non-expressing 25 for his entire life, only being usurped by our ex-Sargent and being sent to high security where he confessed to manipulating everyone around him with his abilities to keep his expression a secret. He even manipulated the brain of his wife to commit suicide. Class 4 nerve impulse manipulation, he's a force to be reckoned with.

I turn up the radio to keep the silence at bay when we ran out of things to talk about. Some time after we left, I think I see a farm, but everything this far out is desolate.

"I think I see the prison," I say, squinting to see some concrete walls in the distance above the corn fields.

"Looks like it," she responds, sitting up in the seat. Some more time passes and the corn fields stop abruptly to give way black concrete buildings and a massive wall ridged up and down, barbed wire and guard towers and all.

I pull into the empty parking lot and the fuel light comes on. "That just used up the rest of the tank," I say, putting the car in collection mode to pull some hydrogen out of the air.

We start on our way to the one-way-in, one-way-out door. It's a 12 foot steel door to allow for some of the larger folks that end up here. There's an inset door for us normal sized people. We walk up to the two guards standing on either side of the doors.

Kekik hands them the manila folder with all our documents to the guy on the right and he simply takes it without a word, turning around to knock on the steel and slides it through, presumably, to someone on the inside.

The sounds of metal on metal sliding about the inside of the door. Complex mechanical noises of bearings shifting around and the doors start opening inch by inch in this awkward silence. Finally it's open enough for us to slip through. It's tight but I'm able to go in sideways only to find more guards on the inside and a foot-thick glass panel with someone at a computer.

"Take these, and you'll be escorted to where your permitted," the lady behind the glass tells us, with a compartment popping open with two internal badges. We take them and a guard motions for us to follow him into the maze of black concrete walls and iron bars.

The place twists and turns and seems completely void of soul until he leads us through a door. The room is reminiscent of the white room at the office. We walk through and the door shuts behind us, and I see a man pacing around behind the glass.

"He's our guy," she tells me. Pale skin, messy blonde hair and beard, C-dampener tightened around the neck.

"I hope your trip was good, officers," he says, shivers going and down my spine.

"My name is Detective Kekik, and this is Detective Olsen," she starts, "We have some questions for you-"

"I should've known that when they said visitors, it'd be cops," he interrupts, "I was a detective once, y'know."

"Yes, I know." Mr. Zeemo scratches his head, and relaxes on the wall behind him, creating an odd tension between the two rooms. Kekik goes on, "Do you remember one detective Jameson?"

He smiles, "Yes, I do."

"Can you confirm that you were the primary factor in his death?" she asks.

"This is, in fact, the first time I've ever been asked that, detective Kekik." I start taking my notes, jotting down his words exactly.

"Answer the question."

"Yes, I killed him; *murdered* him-"

"Were you the primary factor in your wife's death-"

"I've murdered 5 people, detective Kekik: my wife, Jameson-"

"Please just answer the questions I ask." His smile disappears and stares my partner down.

"You're wondering why you're unable to use your ability, aren't you? I can emit an intrinsic-"

"Please remain on topic," she says, stepping up to the glass.

"I'm sorry," he replies, "I've been told I monologue quite a bit."

He goes on to confess the two murders, along with 3 more inside high security. We wrap up with some last formal questions, and we turn to leave. I step out the door and turn back to say something, but the moment she touches the wall, she collapses. The guard rushes to her side, picking her back up, but she collapses again, upturning a little of her stomach on the ground. I go in to help her up too as she coughs.

"What was that?" I ask as we get her to her feet.

"I don't-don't know," she tells me, "But I had a terrible vision; I- just saw decades ahead- I don't-"

"Tell me about it later," I rest her arm over my shoulder and we walk back out. Halfway down the hall she starts walking by herself.

The guard's radio starts chattering about an incident in some sector of the prison and he says we must take a detour through the cells. We pass through steel doors and the sight of the cells is a magnificent feature of prison engineering.

The doors are different, tailored for nearly every individual and to the right are acrylic holding cells elevated from the ground and walls. I step right over some scorch marks from beneath a concrete door.

"What class are most of the prisoners here?" I ask the guard as something strikes against a metal door, echoing in the hall.

"Most prisoners are a class 6," he tells us, "but we have a class 8 in here as well. We pride ourselves about not having a single incident since this prison's conception." I shiver a little at this fact; there's enough power in here to obliterate an entire city down do the soil beneath the foundations.

We make our way to the front and go through the process of leaving the building. I look back at this huge black, ridged building, walking backwards in the empty lot.

I start the car, looking at the fuel indicator, seeming half full, enough to get us to the outskirts of the city. "I think Zeemo forced my ability on me," My partner tells me as we start on our journey back, "It *hurt*, like, badly; I saw decades ahead.

"I saw someone, a villain of sorts, too powerful; and he kept coming back from the dead-"

"Kekik, even in this world, people can't come back from the dead," I try to reassure her, but she's shaken, "Zeemo's a known liar, murderer, he just messed with you to try and-"

"Yeah, you're probably right, there's a lot of different things out there," she starts to relax, "But, damn."

I sit there, looking at the last case connected to the old Sargent update to re-closed and I swipe it away after months of hard work. I get to go back to the grind of city work. Kekik's been spotty recently, saying she's been getting migraines ever since our encounter with Carter Zeemo; he's been reclassified to class 7. We've talked extensively about her vision, she's fixated on it, and not letting go.

"Geez, it's August already," I say to myself, leaning back in my chair. I think to myself, *maybe she's on to something, maybe we're not going to be enough to neutralize a threat?* The federal government, after all, can't enlist 25s for any federal tasks, but the states are left to their own devices, and mine happens to be on the right side of that fence.

My office door opens to see the head of this whole investigation. "Walker!" he greets me, "Well, I'm sure you got the update, but I'd actually like to extend an invitation to join the State Investigation Bureau... Permanently; we could use someone of your talents."

"Oh, what about Kekik, she's probably a better fit." I stand up from my chair and walk over to shake his hand.

"We contacted your partner, but she declined," he continues, "She said she's going on medical leave anywho."

"I accept your offer." he taps my shoulder and walks out of my office. I go back to my desk, and just lean back in my chair; with my job with the state, I might be able to make a proposal for a specialized 25s' division. I open a word processor, and start on something.

I type: The Hero Subdivision.

Cipher

"We've captured the damn criminal, now what?"

I look at this kidnapping psychopath with 3 murders to his name. "Tell us where the kid is!" I shout at him, slamming his head into the steel table.

But all he does is speak in riddles; his mind is too far gone.

"What about using, y'know, the *wizard-*"

"No!" I reject his suggestion, "He's a pompous little ass with his ciphers too."

The criminal lifts his bloody head, "The crane flies alone, while the flamingo stands under the sun and the pigeon is with his flock. The grasshopper dies."

I grab him by his shirt, "Tell us!"

"Give me one of those," I take a puff of a cigarette, looking at the final body. We were too late, too ignorant to listen to the unique way the broken man talked.

The caretaker is scarred beyond repair, and the last child buried in the same yard as the others, but we simply looked over it. I thought I could save at least one.

O' my hubris fails yet another person.

‹‹‐●‐››

Contemplation

The following contains strong themes of suicide.
Proceed if you wish.

SNAP! I wake up from an unpleasant dream, slowly opening my eyes back to reality. I look beside me to find no one laying in bed. I go and get ready for my day; shower, shave, teeth and deodorant.

Today's the day I fly to New York, for something special, or something unique I should say. The flight goes as planned, landing safely against my thoughts on air travel. I find a nice tall building to check into and find a room with my budget for the time being.

There's a restaurant across the street with a special deal with the building, good food too. I walk past a gentleman doing some complicated maths on a napkin. "Hey, I hate to bother, but you seem like a smart fellow," I begin my introduction.

"That what the people say about me," he laughs.

"If you were to drop an object on a rope," I say, "how strong would the rope have to be?"

"Oh, well that depends," he responds. We exchange a few numbers and he gives me the final answer I need.

"Thank you, you're very smart!" I tell the man, going off to eat some food to satiate my ever growing hunger.

"Any day!" he replies, going back to his business.

I stand in this line to the counter, behind a very attractive woman. She turns and waves at me, smiling with a most beautiful smile at me. Time does its signature move and I get to the counter, ordering a sandwich to take to my room.

As I'm in the street, a taxi zooms by, disregarding anything in its path. But I trek onward to my room to enjoy this sandwich in the privacy of my own room. The foyer is busy as I'd expect it to be, and there's a small line to the elevator, surprisingly hosting the cute young lady from the deli.

"Funny seeing you here," she waves to me. I smile back and wait my turn for the elevator, seeing her disappear behind steel doors. Soon I go up to my 3rd-floor room.

I take a bite into my sandwich and realize I forgot to ask for no olives, ruining the wonderful-looking sandwich. I set it to the side and go back to the elevator, waiting to go to the very top floor, but yet again there's a small line.

But I make it up, admiring the premium feel of the upper floor and looking for the door in disguise to the stairwell. I eventually find, being decorated like the surrounding wall, marked with 'Fire Exit'. Up I go to the roof, finding an exercise machine and some rope for *battle ropes*.

I take my time, skillfully tying a not and securing it to the machine, placing the other side around my neck. The steps I take to the edge are expected to be my final. And my last over the edge... *SNAP!*

I wake up from an unpleasant dream, opening my eyes to find a New York hotel room, dark, solely lit through the rising sun behind closed curtains. No one beside me, I go about getting ready for my day; shower, shave, teeth, and deodorant.

There's a deli with a special deal with the building, so I make the commute across the street, being almost grazed by a speeding taxi. I walk past a man doing some complicated maths on a napkin and I come behind a young woman.

She looks behind and smiles with a beautiful smile. "You look familiar, don't you?" she says to me.

"I'm new to the building, but I'm not staying long," I reply.

"Well, enjoy your stay, it's a lovely city," she turns back away and orders and goes away. I order my sandwich and make my way back to my room to enjoy it in privacy.

The street stops for the group of people to make their way across and I walk with them to my building. There's a line for the elevator, but everyone makes it onboard, shouting numbers at the unlucky fellow who happened to be by the panel.

I look around to see the young lady on the other side, but she doesn't see me, and I'd rather not be a bother. Mine's the first stop anyway, so I go off into my room.

When I close the door, I sit down at the desk and open the sandwich, revealing the olives I had forgotten to not ask for. I close it back up and go back to the elevator. I manage to fit in as a larger man steps out and I call out for the top floor.

We make multiple stops, I get there nonetheless. I walk up to the end of the hallway, looking for the stairwell, finding it's decorated like the walls. I walk up the cold stairs to the top and walk out to the roof.

I see workout equipment and a rope. I start tying the rope, carefully securing it to the rest of the equipment and one end around my neck. I take my final steps to the edge until I'm teetering. I take a deep, last breath and take that final step... *SNAP!*

An unpleasant dream wakes me from my slumber, opening my eyes to see my room lit by the sun behind the curtains. I make a plan to go to that deli on the other side of the street, the one with the special deals for hotel occupants.

I manage to walk through the light traffic unscathed and get in line to order the sandwich, behind a cute young lady. She turns her head and smiles very beautifully. "What brings you here?" she laughs, "You look familiar."

"I'm new to the building across the street," I reply, "I'm only here for a short while."

"Well, be sure to enjoy your stay," she tells me before ordering a sandwich, "Oh, and no olives please."

The man nods his head and takes the order and she walks off. "I'll have a number 1, no olives," she reminded me, "thank you."

A time passes and she waves goodbye with her sandwich, and I get mine, losing her to the crowd. I make my way outside and rush to catch the red light for the cars.

I walk to the foyer and see the last of the people walk into the elevator, so I rush to try and catch it. The door almost closes in front of me, but a saving hand reaches through to stop it from closing and the door opens again to reveal the young lady.

"Oh, sorry," she says as I walk in and squish in between some people. She brushes her hair to the side, "Long time, no see."

"Thank you," I tell her, trying to make myself small.

The elevator goes up and reopens on my stop. I walk out and the girl waves goodbye, "Enjoy your sandwich!"

"Thank you," I whisper as it closes. I open the door to my room, sitting down at the desk and enjoy the sandwich. I manage to eat half of the thing, filling me completely. I wrap the sandwich up and place it in the rubbish bin. I look out the window and see that traffic has come to a standstill.

I go back to the elevator and make my way all the way to the top of the building, going to the roof. The door is made to look like the walls but is label as a fire exit.

I look out above the city, the wind blowing underneath my arms. I see the multiple air conditioners bolted to the roof. I walk over to the edge and the wind stops as I look down to my final moments. I take a step... *SNAP!*

I slowly open my eyes, tears flowing down from an awful dream. I look beside me to see no one sleeping with me. I stand up and wrap my head with my hands, but the cold hands gives me no comfort. I go off to get ready for my day; shower, teeth, deodorant.

There's a deli I intend to go to; they have exclusive for building occupants. The cars are speeding past, and it seems that the red light never comes. But it does after a while of waiting. I rush over to the deli to try and secure my place in the queue. I get inside and it looks a little slow. I walk up behind a young miss. "Hey," she exclaims, "You look very familiar!"

"I'm new to the building across the street," I explain, "You may have seen me around there."

"Oh, me too," she says, "I hope your stay is good-"

"Next!" the deli man shouts, hurrying the girl and she gives her order, expressing very harshly, *No olives.*

She makes way for me, and I order a number 1, also expressing no olives. "What's with the olives today," the man says.

I step away for the person behind me. "What brings you to town?" the young lady asks.

"Just visiting for the sake of it," I reply. Another man at the counter calls out for her, giving her her order. Soon the man gives me mine.

"Would you like to walk together?" she insists.

"I'm sorry, I have to go by some hardware soon," I reply, scratching the back of my head, "But I'll see you around the building I guess."

Her countenance falters, "Well, alright. I wish you a good day."

"Thank you," I tell her back. Going off on my way to the hardware store.

The walk wasn't very good against the dusty, cold wind in my face. I come across a homeless man sitting in the street and I tap his foot with mine and set my food beside him for him to eat.

I get inside the store and buy all of the things I need; some rope, a wide door handle, bolts, and a tool. On my way out, I walk by the homeless man with tears of joy, biting down on the sandwich, but I make my way back to my room.

I make my way up the elevator with 5 others, going all the way to the top and to the roof through the brown fire-exit door. I find a good spot to bolt down the hardware and continue to do so.

I haphazardly secure the rope to the hardware and place the noose around my neck. I take the steps to the edge and look back to the opening door. As I fall, I only see the young miss staring back... *SNAP!*

I shoot up from my bed, in a cold sweat and hyperventilating. I reach for a companion only to feel empty sheets. I look to see the sun shining its life-giving ray through the thin curtains covering the window. I stand, and falter, but make my way to the bathroom and wash my face with the ice-cold water from the faucet.

To get my mind off things, I go to the deli at the corner. A car swerves and nearly hits me, but I remain safe. I get in line, behind a woman, her hair is frizzed a little, but she turns and smiles at me anyway.

"Hey," she greets me, "I've seen you around, haven't I?"

"You may have at the building across the street," I reply.

"I think I've seen you there," she persists, "What brings you here?"

"I thought a sandwich would help calm my mind," I tell her, "I don't think I slept that well."

"Same," she tells me, giving me a rundown of her dream, "Strange right?"

"Yeah, totally," I say, before pointing to the counter to let her know she's next.

"No olives, please," she tells the man, "I'm mildly allergic."

"Got it," he replies, motioning to me, "And for you?"

"Number 1, no olives," I tell him, going back to the young lady.

"You don't like olives?" she asks, laughing a little.

"No, never have," I say. We go about talking, laughing. She's spriting and in a good mood, helping me in turn. We get our food and sit down and enjoy the food in each other's company.

"Oh, look at the time, I should get going," she panics, "Walk with me?"

"Sure," I smile back. We make our way back to the building and manage to fit in the elevator. She shouts her floor number and we go up. A few stops later we stop and she gets out on floor 50, while I go straight to the top.

I walk out the elevator and head to the door that leads me to the roof. The wind is calm as I tie my knots on a bolted down door handle, it seems, and tie a knot for myself. I look down at it, ensuring it'll hold. I place it over my head and walk over to the ledge.

The door crashes open and someone runs over to grab my shirt, but it tears away as I fall to my fate. But I look up to see that young lady... *SNAP!*

I scream myself awake; I look around and reach for a companion, grabbing ahold of the sheets and pulling them to me. I look around to desperately find someone, but no one is there, only myself and the sun streaks in the air.

I calm my breathing and open the curtain, looking at the noonday sun shining down on me. Still, I'm not calm, so I go to wash my face, but it seems the pipe froze and nothing comes from the faucet.

I get dressed, tossing on the shirt from yesterday, and make my way to the elevator, faltering in my steps. The door opens revealing an empty elevator. I step inside and press the top floor. My breathing subsides, but my stomach turns and growls at me like a hungry wolf. The elevator stops and opens on floor 50.

A young woman walks in, frizzy hair pulled back, carrying a bag she's holding tight. "Good afternoon," She says to me, "You look oddly familiar, I've seen you around."

"I'm new; I flew in last night."

She smiles at me, instantly calming my nerves; melting away the fright. "I hope you like it here," she tells me, "What floor are you going to?"

"I'm going to the roof actually," I inform her, "To enjoy some nice weather."

She turns her head away from me and brushes a lock of hair away from her face. "Maybe I'll join you later," she presses a button on the panel, making an early stop on the way to the top. We wave goodbye and she goes off into the hallway while I keep going up.

I get on the roof and try to reminisce in the serine weather; sun shining down from the sky. I embrace the familiar rope, shed a tear for this world, and take that step over the edge...

But something grabs me, pulling me away. I smack into the side of the building as this person tries pulling me higher. Finally, they pull me over, crying as I cry, mourning as I mourn.

The young lady holds me tight, saving me from the brink of my purposeful death. We both cry as she drags me back to safety... *SNAP!*

"Babe!" My companion wakes me from my slumber, "Are you okay? You've been shaking in your sleep for, like, twenty minutes."

"Yeah," I say, "Just a bad dream." she sits down next to me on the bed, holding my hand in the sheets.

"Tell me about it-"

"I'm not- it's fine-"

"Please tell me," she persists.

"I'm not going to New York, honey," I reach for her arm.

"You've been looking forward to it for a while," she reminds me of my true intentions, "Are you sure?"

I pull her close and rest my head on her shoulders, crying. "I'm sure." she drops her purse on the bed and embraces me, despite the horrors of my inner mind, she loves me... *SNAP!*

Death of The Dragon King

Sequel to Birth of The Dragon King

I flip through the pages of this book, a book on the nature of subsets of eastern dragons. By manipulating the natural magics, they fly, gliding on ley lines above the sky. They expel energies from their bodies through the same magic.

I'm interrupted by one of my colleagues walking through the door to my office. "Mulan, I have a summons for you," she says.

I look up from my book, sliding in a mark before closing the covers, "Yes, of course. Who is it from?"

"It's a royal summons, m'lady," she hands me the gold-trimmed paper, "Directly from the King."

I roll open the summons, and the King himself has requested my presence as it's been brought to his attention that I'm a leading expert in my field amidst my academic success.

"It says," I pause to read, "There'll be a carriage coming in the morning.

"I hope this'll be good for you, Mulan," she says, "You can't stay and read books forever."

I laugh a little, "Books are how I became such an expert."

"You become an expert by doing, not by candlelight," she says, "You should come with us tonight since you leave in the morning."

"It's rude to sleep in a carriage, so I'll retire to my home."

"Very well, good luck."

I collect my things and attend to my way home, vastly illuminated by the full moon. The way is filled with a nice breeze from the mountain. I've rarely ridden in a carriage, never a royal one.

I arrive to my family's home, walking into the main room seeing my family eating together, my sister, father, and mother. I bow to my parents and leave to go rest.

"Where are you going, Mulan?" my mother calls out to me, stopping me in my steps.

"To bed mother. I leave for the capital in the morning."

My family woos. "Did you find a husband in the capital?"

"No, I've been summoned by the King," I tell them, as I stand in the doorway.

My father grows angry with me, and dawns an angry face, "Why has the *Dragon King* summoned you to the capital?"

"I don't know father," I lie to him, "You're drunk, you need to sleep."

"You bring nothing but misery to me, daughter."

Tears well up in my eye, and I trudge my way to go rest.

The carriage suddenly jumps and jostles as it runs over a stone in the road. And the curtains flow about, leading the sun rays inside. This carriage is furnished with fine things and soft pillows, but it's eery to ride inside alone. I was told the journey should only bee a day, and it's rude to fall asleep. I should've brought a book.

Many hours pass by as the landscape glides across my vision. My mind wanders to my studies, and the fantastic illustrations of dragons that were painted hundreds of years ago. I'm so very glad so many books survived the transition of emperors.

The carriage comes to an abrupt stop and the coachman opens the door. "M'lady, I hope you don't mind, but we must add another guest to the trip."

"Yes, that's fine," I tell him.

"The horses also need to rest," the coachman hands me a small trinket, "When this stops glowing, return to the carriage."

"I look down at my hand to see a small glowing trinket: Magic. My village swore to abandon magic when the Dragon King took power, so I haven't seen much of it since I was a girl. "Yes, I will."

He leads me out of the carriage and I start to explore this quaint town. It's small, but teeming with activity. I fall to my old habits and seek out a book store. I ask the locals for directions and I'm lead to a store. It's small but filled with many unique books.

"Hello!" the storekeeper greets me, "What can I help you with?"

"I'm looking for a book about dragons?" I ask.

"What kind?" he asks back, "How to capture, hunt, an encyclopedia?"

"If you could show me all you have, I would be grateful."

He leads me around the counter and into the back. I look at all the books, some old and new, some with wild designs, perhaps of western origin.

"Here are some," He motions to a shelf, "I have a few editions of Hado here."

"Binding spells?" I ask.

"Yes, mostly spells below 200," he walks over to another shelf, "Here are some encyclopedias."

"Thank you."

I wander the spines of the books and see a few things I haven't seen before, despite the large collection at the school. "What do you know of western dragons?" I ask the shopkeeper.

"I don't know much other than they are no more," he tells me. I look down at my trinket and it grows dim.

I choose a book to read and pull it from the shelf, "I'll take this one." he leads me back and we exchange the goods and go on my way back to the coachman.

I arrive back at the coach and the coachman leads me back in. "Preposterous!" he shouts, "I was not told I'd be traveling with a woman." I look at the man, he's gowned in fine armor with a fine sword beside him.

"I, too, was summoned to the King's presence," I explain.

He laughs, "For what? A concubine?"

"I'm a scholar, an expert on dragons and other mystical creatures."

He scoffs, "Who in their right mind let a woman be a scholar?"

"The Dragon King," I say, making him quiet.

I sit on the opposing side and set my things and my new book beside me. The man's armor is covered in scars and wounds. I do wonder the stories this man can tell, but I don't think he'd tell a woman.

"What's given you so many scars, may I ask?"

He scoffs once more, "War; the Dragon King commands tens of thousands to conquer and unite all of China. I've returned from the battlefield at the King's request," he tells me.

"You look very prestigious."

"I'm a general in the world's greatest army!" he boasts.

I open my book and read about a magical beast known as a Qilin. Lesser creatures who still hold a capable skill of natural magics. They cannot fly, thus easier to capture, but can still expel energies. The illustrations are truly works of art.

This palace is the most magnificent building I've ever seen, I'm in awe; adorned with fine gold, silk, and incredible jade carvings at every corner. Artistic dragon carvings fly around on the walls in every hallway. The flowers bloom all year round, they tell me.

They lead me into the main chamber of the palace, and the general off somewhere else. The doors open to the chamber, and I see many fine tables lining the open space, filled with ornate chairs and other decorations on the tables. None more ornate than the emperor's throne, with two jade dragons leading the arms and a single sculpture winding up the wall behind.

And for a reason unknown to me, a green cushion on the right of the thrown for kneeling. "Why am I led here?" I ask the servant.

"The King has requested to speak with you immediately upon your arrival," he tells me, sliding out a chair for me to sit and wait at the end of the table.

"Do you know why?" I persist.

"That I do not know." I sit down and he slides the chair in.

I look around at the fine luxuries just this room has to offer and ask, "Do you know when he'll arrive, or do I have time to admire this room?"

"By all means," he bows, "All I ask is you don't touch anything."

He exits the room and I admire the metal lining on the wood planks on the table. The back wall has the dragon statue, and it seems as if each and every scale was crafted with a special care. And the antlers befront the dragon are also unique.

"Do you like it?" I hear some man ask.

"Yes," I reply, "It's all so very beautiful." I turn to see the Dragon King himself, dressed in very simple, peasant clothes with holes burned into them, leaving only his bare chest and his coat.

"You must be Mulan, the scholar I summoned."

"Yes, I've study dragons and other mystical creatures for many years now. I actually picked up a new volume on my way here."

"Here at the palace, we have the largest collection of books in China!" he says sitting down very casually next to me, "Books of every kind; in fact, we have many books on mystical creatures, most of which are in perfect condition from the transition of power.

"Have you ever seen a dragon, Mulan?"

"Can't say I've seen any type of mystical creatures in my time."

"Their power is incredible!" he starts waving his hands around, "And they are truly larger than life, that statue testifies nothing of their size."

"You speak as if you've seen one."

He laughs, "You must not know much about me; I've seen one alive, and I killed it, in fact."

"So why summon me?"

"I'm having you help me kill another one."

"I beg your pardon?" I say, confused.

"There's something I so desperately desire, and it's being guarded by a very old dragon. I believe you rode here with one of my top generals in our efforts to bring southern China into the fold; he will be the one to lead the legion to kill this dragon and bring me this thing I so desire."

"Why me?" I ask.

"I've searched far and wide to find someone worthy of this task, and you're a very dedicated individual to your study. I need an expert to go with them.

"And of course, I will take you to wife after this undertaking, seeming if you survive, you'll be worthy of me."

I cough in shock.

It's been several weeks since I arrived at the palace; I've been given access to the palace's entire collection of books regarding dragons. I've been fitted for armor and served with unprecedented luxury I've never before known. The books are magnificent, filled with new information and intricate diagrams on the dissections of dragons.

I've learned so much about dragons in my time here, such that they use natural magics to comprehend human language, something I've never known. Dragons live for hundreds of years, and some hoard great treasures.

Among the books, I've had access to Qilin skeletons and a few dragon bones. Qilins are very similar to dragons, mostly considered lesser dragons, and are more easily captured and studied.

I've been introduced, and largely ignored by many mages and warriors chosen to join the legion and go on this expedition. Magic is not practiced in my hometown, so it's very foreign and strange. The general was not happy to know that I, a woman, would be joining the expedition. He finds we're not fit for war and battle, or anything really.

As every soldier and mage enter the room, I get slowly pushed closer and closer to the back of the room. Then the general in his new armor enters the room, General Gang, and makes his way to the table, rolling out maps and the like.

He points to the mountains to the north and they start strategizing, drawing paths through the mountains with the say of the navigators and the mages. He circles the most likely spot the dragon resides."

"Pardon me!" I try to speak over everyone, pushing past some people, "How is it you're tracking the dragon?"

Someone next to me leans over and explains, "Natural magics change the ley lines. The scouts use special spells to read the ley lines, thus tracking flight paths."

Dragons usually fly extremely high in the sky, "At what altitude do the spells become ineffective?"

"Depends on who's casting them, we have several, very skilled scouts," he tells me, "But even still, it has to be done at key locations.

"Who are you?" he asks.

General Gang starts speaking up above everybody, "The expedition is to commence in 3 days! Prepare yourselves!"

In the 3 days, we all worked tirelessly to pack and prepare our provisions in carts and oxen. But the King himself was nowhere to be found. After all that, it was time to set off into the mountains to fight a dragon and obtain his treasure.

⊷⊙⊶

The men have been murmuring in the poor conditions of the wintery mountains, trudging through the snow and slurry when it rains. We've been knee deeps in snow for four months, and we've come up with nothing. General Gang refuses to listen to anything I have to say because I am a woman; he says I don't belong here with them.

"Gang!" I shout out. Everyone seems to hear me but him. I shout out one more time, but nothing echoes back, not until someone beside him brings me to his attention.

"What do you want, woman?" he barks like a mad dog.

I march up to him, "We've been traveling for four months with no progress-"

"And where would you like us to go, Mulan?" he snarks at me.

I push the man beside him so I can get closer, "There are 2 types of dragons in the North this far-"

"And what about it?"

Furious, I get in front of him, stopping him in his tracks, "They both burrow in the summits!"

"The *mages*, are guiding us through the ley lines-"

I well up in anger and burst, "Clearly!"

He looks down on me, his hardened eyes peering into my soul, "Remember your place, woman-"

"My *place* here is a dragon expert; *you* should remember that."

He turns to address the entire legion, "The woman would like us to go into the mountain's summit to look for the dragon! In the dead of winter! Where the snow will slide out from under us and lead us to our deaths!"

They all start laughing and begin marching around me, further into the mountains. But one stops beside me, "Gang will never listen to you," he says, "But I will, and I can get a mage to listen to you too. I'm Li."

Li starts marching along through the snow as it begins to fall from the clouds. I start my marching again, falling behind with the weak.

Night falls upon us, and one of the mages begin starting fires to keep warm for the night. The fires grow weak and the smoke seems to follow me wherever I sit. Many of the men are praying and preparing for the next day's worth of spells; none of it makes sense to me.

Li approaches me in the night and sits down beside me. "If you think you can find the dragon hiding in these mountains, I can help you up the mountain, and one of the mages will come as well."

"We'd be separated from the legion, though."

"The mage will be able to lead us back."

I begin to meditate on the knowledge within my head. All that I read in preparation. The dragons that once dwelt here either burrow deep within the mountain or hide in the summit. The mages are certain that all the mountains we've been adjacent to do not hold the dragon.

"It'll take too long to find the burrow in these conditions," I tell him.

"If you're confident in which mountain, the mage will help us with that too," Li replies.

"It's dangerous-"

"If you keep making excuses, then we can just suffer for a year trying to find it. The magician will come at midnight, so don't sleep."

The magician flips through his little book atop this mountain, "I'm sensing flight patterns going that way."

"Both types of dragons live up at the summits, correct?" Li asks.

"If we can get higher up," the mage says, "I'd be able to get better results."

Li looks up at the moonlit summit, "The snow would be too much, it's fresh, not packed."

The mage closes his spell book, "I have something for that."

Li rubs his face to think, "Alright, Mulan, you better be right about this."

The magicians start drawing lines in the snow, drawing an intricate, delicate, precise image. "The mages are going to lead the legion further north, but I'm reading flight patterns to the east."

The mage pulls on Li's and my hands, putting my hand on his forearm. The mage begins whispering an old dialect, and suddenly I'm pulled through a spell with a blinding flash of light like I'm pulled by a speeding horse.

I fall back and sink into some cold, soft snow with a spinning head. I try to stand, but I keep sinking further into the snow; each step I take I sink further down. "Mulan!" Li calls out, as I start talking to myself, "Just stay calm and you'll sit still."

The mage shushes both of us, right before the snow compacts down in an instant, freezing my legs still, but freeing my torso. Li reaches out and I'm able to climb out to my feet.

I wrap my arms around myself in this even colder weather atop the mountain. "Do you see any signs of the dragon?"

I try to focus and look atop the mountain, but I see nothing; no signs of the dragon here. Li says he hasn't found anything unusual either in or beneath the snow.

The mage makes us jump from one mountaintop to another, all night until the sun rises. And Li finally sees something unusual. The mage tells us all the magic flows into this one mountain, but I look and don't see the burrow.

The haze of the legion is off in the distance. Gang has already probably noticed that we've deserted, but I doubt that he cares very much, he'll probably assume us dead to the King.

The sun begins to peek from beyond the horizon, which means the legion is already on their way north. I walk to the mage, sinking into the snow one step at a time. "Not again," I say to myself.

"Stay right there, don't move!" Li shouts, holding his hand out to stop me, "I think it's hollow underneath here." he pulls out his sword, and pushes it into the snow. It keeps going down and down and doesn't stop and I think I hear a small echo beneath my feet.

"It's definitely hollow underneath," he whispers, "We have to let the legion know-"

The snow gives way and I fall through into the burrow. I hit the cold, hard stone, and my armor clangs, echoing through the hole leading deeper in the mountain. I rush to my feet, making even more metallic ringing noises, trying to dig through a layer of ice with my frozen fingers to no avail.

"Who goes there?" I hear a wispy, elderly voice call out form the deep. In fear, I pull out my sword and break through the ice, continuing digging through the snow to get out.

Snow starts falling, burying me as I try to escape the burrow, but somebody grabs onto my hands and starts pulling me through. I feel a presence slithering towards me, something dark and fear to instill. *WHOOSH!* It arrives upon me, but I'm pulled back out into the open.

I stop my hyperventilating, and roll to face the sun. "There's a dragon in there, I know it."

"Let's return back to the legion."

We finally reach the legion after hours of marching through the snow. I'm exhausted, ready to collapse. "Halt!" General Gang holds up his fist. I stop and fall to my knees in the snow.

"The deserter has found the dragon's burrow!" Gang announces, "We shall bring it down by evening!"

The legion starts to murmur, and Li lifts me by the arm to get me back to my feet. He brings his hand up, and does a little trick, revealing a small magical trinket. "Hold this in your hands, it'll warm them up."

I take it, and encapsulate it in my hands and feel it's warmth going into my frozen, blueish fingers. The legion starts marching in a different direction, and I begin to trudge along with them.

I find the sun to be directly overhead, but it withholds its life-giving heat. The 4 months we've been out here have landed us in winter where the cold wind blows upon the desolate mountains.

We arrive at the mountain before the sun sets, we have plenty of time for the battle inside the burrow. Some of the mages up the mountain to put down anchors so we can climb up. The soldiers begin tying ropes against our armor.

General Gang approaches me, "You're going first, *dragon expert.*"

The people around him begin to laugh as if they're leading a mad cow to death. The soldiers they the end of the rope around me, push and lead me along to the base of the mountain. They just keep pushing me along until I'm all the way at the first anchor. The first mage bows and motions the way I'm supposed to go.

Angrily, I put the trinket in my mouth and grab the lead up the mountain. I pull against the rope, rashing my hand. I pull again and march up the mountain, step by step. "Heave!" I shout, pulling myself up the mountain in a rhythm. Soldiers begin following after me, in the rhythm. "Heave!"

My cold hands start leaving blood on the ropes as I keep marching up the mountain as my palms are rashed raw, but we reach the burrow. I see the hole I left when climbing out. The air is freezing up here, freezing the blood on my hands. One of the mages behind me climbs up too, casting a spell and *BOOM!* the snow blasts away down the mountain, revealing the burrow.

I draw my sword and the mage pushes behind me, forcing me to march into the burrow. Step by step I walk inside, with the feeling of fear and stiff air returning.

"Why are you here?" I hear the wispy voice say once again, which a gust of warming wind blowing down the burrow.

We blaze deeper until the light disappears from the burrow and the legion is left in darkness. The mages cast light spells on the walls and they glow like torches.

I look down at a shimmering item on the floor, finding it to be a silver coin. I find another and follow the trail to a torn bag next to a skeletonized corpse. The trinket in my mouth grows cold and I pick it out, putting it in my pocket.

The air grows warm, and my finger regains their color as we go deeper. I keep finding more and more corpses of varying preservation.

"Has another legion been led to their doom?" the voice says, but it's no longer wispy, but as if it were a man talking to me face to face. I get shivers as I feel something approaching, quickly. Before I know it, I'm smashed into the wall by a great beast.

I see a white and blue beast swirling around the burrow, knocking the legion around into the wall. It swirls in chaotic curves throughout the air, smashing back and forth, which only the mages dodging the dragon. The battle that ensued was glorious and hard won.

The dragon struggles against the Hado spells restraining it to the wall. Men have died in this battle, but I hope we have won. I fall to my knees in exhaustion, holding myself up with my sword in the ground. I look at my hand, bloodied with my own blood and the blood from the wounded dragon.

"What is your name?" General Gang asks the beast. The dragon responds by expelling fire from its mouth, heating up the air once more. "Very well, I suppose it's not important.

"Find a golden hilted sword with scaled scabbard and bring it to me!" he commands the survivors.

I pull myself up to my feet and wander deeper into the burrow. It's hot and humid inside here. Step by step, a feel a small breeze gently caress me and guide my steps. The whispers of what is possibly the arcane language of nature draw me closer to a pile of gold and silver.

I climb, and falter, but climb the pile all the way to the top. "Mulan has found it!" I hear Li shout back to the surviving legion.

All the whispers arrive at this sword, resting at the top of this mound. I grasp the hilt and the whispers echo into oblivion. I hold the sword and slide down the mound, making my way to the General.

"Good, woman," Gang says, "You've found it."

"This?" I say, coming to my senses, "This?!"

"Men died for *this*?!" I shout.

"Calm down, woman!" Gang shouts at me, holding out his hand.

I unsheathe the sword, ready to challenge Gang, but nothing but iron dust and fragments falls from the hilt and scabbard. I stare down at the sword in horror. Men died for this worthless pile of dust?!

I fall down to my knee, and start wailing; I watched men die for this. I cry out in pain, and I hear the dragon call out too. Tears flow down my face, and a cold breeze blows around me and my armor.

"Why are you crying?" I hear a woman say.

"Because-" I can't make the words come out, "People died!"

"People die all the time," she says, "it's the circle of life-" I cry out once more, wailing. "But you're not used to seeing that, are you?"

I look up to find this woman, and I see her, dressed in fine clothes sewn with gold and a wonderful fenguan. She sits there behind a small table with a cup in her hand, filled to the brim, nearly spilling over.

"Won't you join me for some tea-"

I begin to panic, "Where am I?" I look around and find myself at the base of a mountain, green with trees and other jungle flora. There's a waterfall not too far in the distance. "How did I-"

"*You* are still in my husband's burrow," I turn around to see a mirror, showing me the legion surrounding me; *me*, frozen with the sword wrapped by my arms in my bosom. "Your soul is here in my soul's realm; lovely isn't it? It reminds me of home.

"You've awoken my soul inside that sword," she points to the item in my hand, clean and pristine, "Those who do so, I will offer great power-"

"I don't want great power- I'm a scholar, not a soldier."

"Really?" she takes a sip of her tea, but it remains full, "You're the first one in centuries to not accept that offer.

"Tell me," she asks, "Why did you seek my sword?"

"I was forced to join a legion as an expert to guide them to it." I set the hilt on the ground and sit by the table, realizing my cup is empty.

"Who commands the legion?"

"A man named General Gang, but he was ordered to retrieve it for the Dragon King," I tell her, setting the cup back down on the table.

"A Dragon King, you say?" she sets her cup down as well, "Why is he called such?"

"Legend says he slew a dragon named Yohan and their souls became one," I explain.

"And this is what I offer you, though less *permanent*," she says, "Is he a good king?"

"I'm not sure."

We sit in silence for a few moments, I look around, admiring the landscape I've never been privileged enough to see. "Let me make you the offer again," she says, "I offer you all my power if you wield this sword."

"And in return?" I ask.

She laughs, "You're different than your predecessors. In return, you offer me senses back into the mortal world.

"As magnificent as I've crafted this world to be, it doesn't satisfy my desires." I look upon her one more time and see a woman who's been trapped in a box for far too long.

"I accept your offer," I say, "I will give you the senses you desire."

"And my great power?" she asks, "You could use it to overthrow this *Dragon King*. After all, if you don't know if a king is a good king, he's most likely not a good one- in my experience."

I stop to think about this offer and everything that is; all I wanted was to study books until the day I die, but now I'm thrown into all this. "I'm reluctant," I say, "But I accept."

"Our contract is sealed."

In renewed vigor and strength, I stand back up on my feet. I feel burning, yet comfortable. My reflection on Gang's armor reveals flames coming from inside of my armor, blazing from the seams. I point the hilt at Gang, and a blue flame, sharp as a blade, begins to emit from the hilt.

"Gang!" I shout, rushing up and swinging the sword across his chest, tearing his armor into pieces. Gang falls on his back, baffled, whilst I march past him, marching past everyone in shock from the flames coming from me.

The dragon squirms pinned to the wall, breaking free of some of the Hado bindings. "No!" The dragon shouts, filling the burrow with noise.

I make my way to the entrance and the sun has gone away behind the horizon. The moon is crescent, and I summon the power of the dragon within and the flames to engulf me, picking me up from the ground and whipping across the sky, riding the ley lines and flying.

We glide high above the snowy mountains below, the view is breathtaking. I see the woman flying beside me, smiling. I hear her voice clear as day over the wind rushing past my ears, "It's so wonderful to see the world once more."

The mountains go away in the distance as I approach a village, glowing in the night beneath the moon. I see the roads leading into the distance and begin to follow the path back to the capital.

I start spiraling down to the inner doors of the palace. It draws closer as the fire around me burns brighter. The sun peeks up from the east, and I crash through the doors.

CRASH! The doors burst into pieces, wood and metal scattered across the hallway. I stand back up, putting the sword back in its scabbard and extinguishing the flames. I brush the debris off of me, and to the surprise of the guards in shock and awe, I march down the hallway, heading towards the main chamber of the palace.

"M'lady," a man in silk robes tried to stop me amidst the doors to the chamber, "The Dragon King is having a banquet-" I swing the scabbard across his face, knocking him out onto the floor.

I push on the finely decorated door, but it's barred from the other side. I whisper the dragon within this sword, "Grant me your strength-"

I draw the sword and as the flames reengulf me, I strike the door with the blue flame. It leaves burning embers crackling on the door. The woman appears next to me, "It appears to be guarded with a spell." She snaps her fingers, and I feel something innate drawn out of me with the beating of a drum, like a single heartbeat in my ear.

Nevertheless, I strike the door again, the intense flames forcing the door to crumble, and in its wake, I am revealed. The crowd eating and being merry amongst the tables falls silent. I march through, the folk making way for me.

"Xin Li!" I shout out, calling for the King. He sits upon his throne with a man in fine robes sitting at his side. I grab the hilt with both hands and the flames burn even hotter, yet I feel no pain.

"Mulan," he stands, with the man to his side transforming into a dragon and flying into the Dragon King's body, "You dare threaten me in my home? After everything I've offered you-"

I scream, running forward sword in hand. Gang, wearing his utterly broken armor, and a mage magically appears between us, stepping from the interspace. "Woman!" she shouts, attempting to grab the sword from me, but I kick him away, and the mage backs off.

"Gang, let me handle this," the Dragon King tells him, followed by Gang crawling away from us. "Do you want to fight, Mulan?" he raises his hands and flames crawl around the floor, surrounding the two of us in a wall of heat.

We circle each other, waiting for the other to strike first. I'm impatient and rush forward at him, but he snatches the sword from me and kicks me down. The power drains from me and the fire begins to burn me and cook me inside my armor.

"Just as I thought this would go," he turns around, looking at the sword in depth.

I reach out my hand, "Return to me." Blue flames surround the King and the hilt comes flying back to my hand. Flames engulf me once more, relieving the burning feeling.

"I'm impervious to fire," he reminds me, "It'll come down to how long you can last, either, without your sword or my strikes."

"Impervious to fire?" the woman whispers, "No one has such ability." she giggles and the blue flames grow stronger, glowing as bright as the sun.

My armor melts away, pooling at my feet. I scream, running forward ready to attack. The Dragon King readies his fists in a martial arts stance, and the blue dragon formed of fire comes swirling from the hilt. The blue flame swirls around his stance and bites on his neck.

A dragon formed of red fire flies from his mouth, chaotically flailing about before aiming itself at me.

I stand victorious, the banquet's guests staring in horror at me and the dead king. His corpse has been burned down to the charred bones, and me myself am covered in burns, but I stand alive and the successor to the throne by law. I suppose I've become queen one way or another.

I look around, placing the sword in the scabbard and the flames disperse. "My my, look at you, my warrior woman," the woman says to me. My feet take their steps to the throne. I scream, slashing the sword and destroying the throne and the jade dragon behind. The crowd starts to panic and disperse out of the hall.

General Gang looks in horror while he's still on the ground. "Leave me, Gang, and never come back," I mutter, and he turns tail and runs away in fear.

"What is your name?" I ask her, sitting on the platform the throne once stood.

"Call me what you like," she kneels down next to me on the cushion, "What is your name?"

"Mulan," I tell her, as I begin to cry, "Queen of China."

I take a sip of my tea, upon my throne with my friend beside me, the dragon. The doors open to the main chamber, and two guards and a mage walk through with a special guest as I summoned them.

"This is a nice place," I hear our guest say, "Fancy stuff, unlike the King's." The magic between us translates his western language and my language into something we both can understand.

"You've caused quite a mess in the west, I hear," I tell him.

"I can assure you, the mess has been taken care of."

"Ilus Everaurd, he who killed the pest, Milo, leader of the Black Hands," I announce, "I have need of your skills."

Demons

A sequel to Angels

Here I am, face to face with the man who hates me the most: Mr. Free, or that's what they call him. The scars on his face from Martta are clear as day, a reminder to himself of pure hatred. The room is cold, white concrete scrubbed clean every day. Air conditioning is crank as high as the budget allows.

"Despite my *best* efforts," he goes on, "You have impressed upon my superiors that this mission is a viable option for diplomacy between our two societies."

"Yes sir," I reply.

"*Yes, sir,*" he mocks me, "I've handpicked the people going with you to beyond the portal."

"I was informed that I-"

"You were informed wrong," he juts, "I'll be counting the days you're out of my sight. You are dismissed."

I turn sharply and walk out of the room, turn the corner and make my way to my personal space. I pass by another patron who hates me dearly for some unknown reasons.

"Attention!" I hear my superior shout as he walks down the hall. I stiffen up and face the other wall. One by one, he taps some of our shoulders, signifying we need to follow him. He passes by me, lightly touching my shoulder and I stiffly walk behind him down the several halls to our destination.

Lone and behold, it's yet another concrete room in this underground prison. "Y'all can relax now," he commands us, allowing us to take some seats. I look beside me and see that other young man sitting with us.

"You've all been briefed on this assignment," he says, "You've been chosen to go beyond the portal: to another world to make peace with some savages."

He flips on a projector, with some photos from our side of the gate; a time lapse of them building a structure around their end of the portal. Slow, stone by stone, then black. In the last frame, I catch a glimpse of a single-horned demon I know.

"They have attempted to block us out after our last attempt at diplomacy, building a stone structure all around," he says, turning off the projector. He flips through some folders sitting on a rack, pulling a few out. "Y'all's job is to push through the barrier and make contact with the demons and establish good relations."

In asynchronous unison, we repeat, "Yes, sir!"

BANG! BANG! I fire shots at a target in the range, all next to my new colleagues, one of which I still have yet to have a decent conversation with. I've been informed that my local persona is that of a traitor; despite my previous records being sealed, word got around of my connection with Martta. *BANG! BANG!*

A few more shots empty my magazine, and I set my gun down, staring at the manufacturing label: Panzer Manufacturing. I take a deep breath in and out, letting the gunpowder burn my nostrils. The target comes speeding back at me, revealing my shots. *Eleven out of twelve isn't bad*, I think to myself. I pull the paper form the hook and roll it up, pack it in my back pocket.

"Another briefing today, James," someone says to me.

"Yeah, seven sharp," I reply. We shake hands and part ways for the rest of the afternoon. I open my locker and start flipping through the folder I was given. A large part of the things in here I heard first hand from Martta, another is speculation from observation on our side of the gate.

Martta once told me that she was created from a human mother, and her father was presumably one of the large humanoid silhouettes; wings and horns like something you'd see in the movies.

I close the folder and start carrying it all back to my quarters. *It's him, that guy*, I hear people whisper as I walk past them, but I pay no attention until one of them runs into me, shoving me to the side.

"Watch where you're walking," they say, walking off. I let it go and keep walking to my quarters.

I open the door and see my roommate. We keep a silent relations between us. Everything on my side is still in order, but his side is always some sort of a mess. The clock ticks down until it hits seven and I hear a knock on my door on the dot.

"James!" I hear, "It's time to move!"

"Yes!" I shout back, grabbing my jacket and start walking to the briefing. The hallways are cold and sharp, you can nearly cut yourself on the corners.

I arrive to see 5 others sitting there in chairs and a projector shining on the wall. "We can begin," Mr. Free says.

"Yes sir," I say, sitting down.

"Let's begin," he says, flipping the slide on the projector, "With our previous attempts at diplomacy, we know there's a central leader of some kind, but they've stayed in the shadows.

"There's one code-named the *Icon of Sin*, who seems to be one of their leaders," he flips the slide to a hazy silhouette of a massive beast with beast-like legs.

"We have the database of hybrids that have been on Earth in some military action against us, but we put that to rest," He flips through a collection of pictures, one including Martta, "And for the first time in human history, *we* will cross the portal to try and make peace with them.

"We have someone in our midst who has good relations with the other side, so he's been chosen, *against* my best efforts, to lead you on this mission."

Everyone in the room looks my way. "Let us continue on," Mr. Free says, "The environment is low in nitrogen, but high in oxygen and carbon dioxide. It *is* breathable, but you'll need time to adjust, according to our estimates."

I pull the straps on the uniforms we're using for the mission. Oddly comfortable, made from an ugly green and rugged fabric; lots of place for clips and whatnot. "How's it feel, James?" the outfitter asks me.

"Good," I reply.

"Let start packing on body armor." she lugs some new armor, designed for more primitive weapons, like spears and maybe arrows. All our data shows they don't have modern weapons. Martta told me they didn't even have glass.

"Mhm?"

"Yeah, fit's good," I say. She keeps stacking on more until it's all on, adding another some-odd 50 pounds. I do a squat up and down to make sure it's not too heavy, I haven't had a whole lot of time to exercise. The mirror shows ugly green and brown, and for the life of me, I can't think of a reason to go camouflage.

The others are going through the same process, but no one wants to speak with me aside from the mission briefings. I look around and everything seems to be in order for everything.

Rick seems to avoid me at all costs, even being on the other side of the room whenever we're in the same place. Mr. Free walks in, in his loose-fitting suit and tablet.

"I hope everything is fitting correctly," he says with his cold, brutal lips.

"Yes sir!" we all say, not even close to the same time.

"Good," he replies to all of us, "The clock ticks ever closer." he taps his wrist and leaves us. Everything seems to be in order, so we all start taking off the armor and leaving it to the outfitter. One of the boys slaps the hand of the outfitter, making her drop it to the floor. They walk by and Rick shows me the bird as he walks out.

We kneel down and pick up the things. The rest of the outfitters walk out as well as I hand her the armor and whatnot. "Thank you," she says as the others walk out, leaving the two of us.

We stand up and I leave her to her work, saying, "No problem."

I get to my quarters and see a folder lazily jammed into my locker. I start pulling, ripping part of the folder, but eventually getting it out. It reads about a rover that was sent successfully through and back. Previous attempts failed because the 'fields' or something rather was too chaotic for electronics to survive the trip. The newest one had to be controlled using visible light.

There are apparently several rovers lying there to retrieve for the government. The one that *did* make it through bored a hole through the wall they made was destroyed in minutes by guards of the keep. Not before a picture was taken of human-demon hybrids. One of dark complexion and another with blonde hair with wings to match.

Good to know that we might be met with resistance.

BANG! BANG! I slide the magazine in and out with new bullets, emptying the new cartridge. 12 out of 12, deviation of only a couple of inches. I start breathing again as my target comes speeding to me. I look at the gun, making sure it's mine: Panzer Manufacturing; it's nearly the sole weapons manufacturing company used by this division of the military.

I scratched a line underneath the serial number to mark it as mine, a common thing to do among us, carving patterns into the handle. Tomorrow's the day we go over to do our mission, I've seen all the equipment packed in heavy, shielded containers being shipped all the way up to the portal.

I set my gun back into the locker and head off for, what I think, the night to sleep. I lay down in my bed as the lights go off. Something wakes me in the night. The ground shakes and the walls have their dust thrown off. I jump to my feet, reaching for the knife that's supposed to be on my nightstand, but isn't.

The locker bursts open and slowly a burning red horn creeps out, and I see Martta, hissing like a beast. Her other horn, blackened, peeps out as her whole head comes into view. Striking yellow eyes looking my way. She leaps at me, waking me up from my nightmare.

"You good?" My roommate asks, "You've been making noises for the past hour and you *just* screamed."

"Yeah- I'm-" I catch my breath, "Good lord, it's hot in here."

"Not really," he persists, "I think you've been worked up for tomorrow."

I slow my breathing, standing up to look into the locker. I slide the lock and look inside, seeing the extinguished carvings of her horn laying there on the shelf, right where I left it. My heart is beating so loud, it drowns the draft of air from the vents.

"Good?" my outfitter asks me, strapping the last of the body armor on.

"Good," I reply. She steps away and I get handed my handgun and my rifle, whilst putting them on my body. Finally, she hands me an oxygen converter to put in my mouth.

We all line up and start marching forward. The glass doors open and the portal comes into view. It's larger than I remember, but it's still a cube. The stone walls on the other side are there just like the briefings said and multiple rovers just sitting there on the other side.

One by one, we heave the containers containing food, ammunition, and other amenities for us on the other side as we won't be making the trek back until a clear failure, success, or maybe for a restock.

We set the first one on the wheels and start pushing it through with a wooden stick. It enters the threshold and the metal starts whining a high pitch sound all the way through it, only shutting down to a muffle once it's through.

I bring the wooden pole to my face, smelling the charred surface. Again we push the next one through, and again until we finish and the last one is on the other side. We hand away from the wood poles and line up once again.

"You'll want to pass through as quickly as you can, without running," we hear over the intercom.

Everyone nods and looks at me, as if I'm supposed to go first, but I know better to fight it and start rushing forward. Step after step I draw closer and I'm reminded of Martta's last encounter with me. I nearly trip, but I catch myself and pass through the threshold of the portal.

I feel, briefly, like I walked into an oven all over my body, but it quickly subsides as I'm through. I pat down my body to make sure I'm not on fire and burn my finger on my gun. I take a deep breath in through the converter, breathing in the rich oxygen atmosphere. My head gets a little light, but I keep my repose.

I give a thumbs up and the next guy rushes through, and the next until Rick jumps through last. I look around the portal and see the rest of the failed rovers. I hear some chattering, not sure if it's from the portal or outside the wall.

I look through the portal and see some guy in a lab coat holding up a piece of paper, reading, "Get the rovers now." A thick cord with a hook comes flying through and landing right before me. I give a thumbs up and hook it on the first rover as they pull it through.

It took an hour or so to pull them all through, the rest of the boys just standing there, loading their guns. One of them pulls out the hammer to bust the wall down. The closer inspection looks like clay holding together the stones, so it shouldn't be a hassle to bring it down.

THUD! Henry smashes a hold right through it, popping out a stone. The chattering becomes more clear and I hear footsteps running off in the distance. *THUD!* Another few stones fall away.

"No!" I hear someone shout from the other side. I almost forgot they speak English. A spear flies through one of the holes. "Go back!"

Everyone looks at me, forcing me to do all the work. I take another breath and take out my oxygen converter. "We're, uh-"

"No!" the spear gets pulls back, "Go back!"

"No, we're here for-"

"We *don't* care!" he shouts.

Rick comes up next to me, "We're heavily armed and we have superior defenses; you can't stop us." I wave my hand, signaling 'Don't'.

"I'm, uh- I'm here to see Martta," I say, "Do you know who I'm talking about? And Kiira?"

"No!"

I catch my breath from the new atmosphere, "Yes! We're not leaving-"

"Then die!" the spear flings right past my face through the hole. Henry thwacks the wall and breaking another hole in it. The spear retracts and the final blow to the wall brings it down.

We come face to face with the demon, reddish skin and curly hair. He brandished his spear and Rick pulls out a gun. I pull it down and he fires, casting the bullet at his feet.

"Diplomacy," I remind him, "That *is* what we're here for.

"Put the gun away," I whisper to him, "I'm leading here." reluctantly, I know, he puts it back in its holster.

The spear comes flying past the two of us. With my quick thinking, I catch it. "No! Get away-"

"No, you!" I shout, digging the spear into the ground, "We're not here to fight." I look around to see everyone's hands on their guns. I wave my hand at them to relax.

The demon walks up to me and shoves me back, "All you ever want to do is fight!"

"Not this time," I raise my hands, "We're here to make peace with you guys."

The sky here really is green, bird-like things with two sets of wings: the *Yousi*. There are three suns; two yellow, a large and a small; and a red sun. I've counted 2 moons in the sky as well.

"You wait here," he points to the ground. He's lead us up a stone brick building without any windows, held together by clay and medium-sized stones just like the wall around the portal. He goes in through some *wooden* doors that are 10-ish feet tall.

Mostly, everything about the village that surrounds this one building are tent huts and stone wells. Tallgrass stretching across the distance and yet nobody walking about, probably hiding from us. I don't recall seeing any trees either.

"So, uh," Henry says, taking out his converter to adjust to the air. He coughs a little before breathing deep, "Damn, this is clean air!

"Anyway, do you really trust these things?"

"They're half-human, Henry," I tell him, "Yes, I trust these people."

Rick scoffs and says something under his breath, but I pay no attention to it. The wooden doors open and a familiar face greets me with a new eye-patch. I rush up to shake Kiira's hand.

"Hey! You must be Kiira! I'm James, We're here on a diplomatic-" she starts squeezing my hand harder and harder, causing me a sharp pain from my bones hitting each other, "Ow, okay."

She lets go and starts sniffing the air. "I smell betrayal," she whispers to me.

"Anyways-"

"No anyways," she stops me, "You know you're not welcome here."

"Kiira," I back away and say aloud, "We're here for diplomacy, we want to make peace between our two societies-"

"No," she states, "You're not welcome here." she waves her hand around, "Do you see anybody? It's because we don't want you here; everybody is hiding from you.

"You come here with weapons and talk peace," she goes off, marching towards us as I back away to keep distance, "I know what you use those for, not *peace*."

I look over my shoulder to see Rick holding aiming his pistol. "Rick!" I shout, "Diplomacy isn't a shooting target!"

"I *feel* threatened, James," he shouts back.

"I'll show you threatened," Kiira rushes up to us, bearing claws.

I jump between them, with Rick's guns poking me in the back. "Diplomacy, dammit!"

"No, you're right," Ricks says, slowly placing the gun back on his hip. Kiira backs away looking through me to Rick.

"So, Kiira," I try to bring the train back on tracks, "We have official documents to read to you guys-"

"That's not how we work over here," she cuts me off.

"What- what do you mean?"

"Thanks to your war on us," she begins, "We formed a council."

"A council?"

"Of the leaders of *our* world," she explains, "And they will not see you."

Rick gets out from behind me, "We've invested *resources* to be here."

"They won't see you," she persists, facing me, "*Harru* came rushing in, saying you were here. The ones that are here agreed to send you back."

"How many councilmen do you have?" I ask.

"8 from this landmass, the others refused to join."

Rick starts waving his hands, "We're not leaving until we complete the mission!"

"Rick," I shove him back, "But he's right, we have a lot riding on this, I have to insist."

She eyes us down, counting us I think. "*James*, come here," she pulls me along.

She whispers to me, "They *will not* see them, but he might see you."

"Okay?"

"You need to stay out for a few days while I talk to them."

"Jeez, we have a lot to catch up on," I turn my head to see Rick staring at us.

"No," she says, "We don't."

The two yellow suns set, leaving the red sun walking the horizon. There's so much we could teach them, like concrete, for one thing, to fix all these weak structures. This could open a whole new field of astronomy and science. Everything is riding on this.

The flashlight flickers, but it's fairly lit outside from the red sun. Everyone's joking around, eating MREs. Some of the townspeople are out and about, some of them coming within viewing distance, standing above the tallgrass. Most of them look very different than Martta and Kiira; some have red skin, some have dark skin, but they all have a variety of horns and wings.

I look back to see the one from earlier who led us into town, approaching us with a spear in hand. "I've been told to watch you."

Rick cocks his gun, showing the gold plating off to the boys. "Well, don't be a stranger and relax a little," Ricks says to him.

"No," he persists on being stiff, "I watch you." ricks shrugs his shoulders and continues talking with everyone else.

I get and start to walk to him, but he mounts his spear. I move forward slowly, keeping my hands up. "Harru, right? I just want to ask some questions-"

"No!" He pokes the spear at me, "I watch."

"I just want-"

"No!" he shouts.

"Very well," I go back to sitting on the ground and finish off my MRE. He just stands there for the rest of the time until we all finally pass out.

"So what are we doing with the cargo?" somebody asks me.

"Keep it by the access point in case of failure. I don't want to go through the effort of moving it closer if we fail," I command, "Mark and Trevor, go get the water extractor and come back."

"Yes sir," they reply, turning tail and making the trek back.

"What about him?" Henry points to Harru sleeping on the ground, "I've afraid he'll stab me if I wake him up."

"They *are* strong," Rick says, "I'm questioning the choice of body armor."

"I'll do it," I say, walking up to him and picking up the spear so he doesn't immediately attack. I tap him a little with my foot and he flinches, shooting up to his feet and readies his claws at me. I just raise my hands and toss him the spear. He looks at me and then his spear, inspecting it.

"Oh, hey, Trevor!" I yell out to them, "Start putting down anchors!" he gives me a thumbs up from the distance.

"Where are they going?" Harru says, "I need to watch you all."

"They're going to get some water for us," I tell him, "We can all wait here for them to return, shouldn't be an hour?"

"Hour?" he sounds confused but shakes his head to refocus.

I've noticed the two yellow suns are perpendicular to the horizon, but the red sun is almost parallel to it, only dipping below after all this time.

"I watch all of you," he persists.

"How about this?" I try to diffuse him, "You take us back, and send another out to the- the, uh." I pause trying to think of a good, non-technical word. "Um, *portal,* to bring the two back."

He narrows his eyes, and points at me, "I don't like it."

"Well?" he turns around and starts walking toward the big stone building in the distance. A lot of the tallgrass is cut into paths slithering around the flat landscape. I look around to admire the lack of clouds or mountains.

Harru starts shouting in his own language and pointing around until another couple of natives go running off into the distance. They run past us, going on the trail.

"Where are we even going?" Rick blurts out.

"I watch you," Harru responds.

"No, I mean-"

"I watch you," he persists.

"I don't think he speaks good English," Henry tries to say. Some of the other boys start roughhousing a little, but Rick breaks them up.

We approach the stone and clay building at the center of it all. Harru stops us but remains silent while we all try to figure out what's going on. I check my watch, it being automatically adjusted for the shorter, more complicated day cycle; it has a fancy watch face that tells me the positions of the suns, custom from a watch company. Rick's, of course, is gold.

"Harru," I try to get his attention, "What's going on?"

"We wait," he responds, looking away, leaning on the wall.

"Why again didn't we bring coms?" Rick retorts.

Henry catches the attention, "We wanted to remain undisturbing to the environment as much as possible."

"And radio waves would've messed with that?" Rick continues.

"It was too much of a risk to take," I tell him, "I think I see Trevor in the distance."

I start waving to Trevor, and his 3 companions walking in the distance, they've made good time. They stop and hammer in another anchor, but the two demons start bickering over it. Harru starts shouting at them in their language. After a few minutes, they catch up.

One of the demons in the half-human variety, the other is a native: they have brownish-red skin, dark eyes, normal-looking feet; antlers of all things popping out of the straight, black hair.

"You," Harru pokes me in the back with his spear to get my attention. I turn around and see Kiira walking through the door.

"*James*," she says to me, "Harru brought you back successfully." she pulls me aside, and I catch a glimpse of Rick eyeing me down. "*He* has agreed to see you, but only you."

"Who?"

"King Borro," she informs me, "He rules this country, and leads the council."

"Sounds like a big deal," I confess, looking back at the group, "When will he see me?"

"He's inside," she says, "*Alone.*"

"That's intimidating," I tell myself, "I need my bag-"

"No, you have to leave everything outside."

I call Henry over and hand him my rifle, looking at Kiira. "That too," she points to my pistol. I hand that over to Henry too, him having a shocked look on his face with the rest of the boys laughing about to themselves.

Kiira opens the door enough to slide through, and motions that I go inside.

The door closes behind me, and there are sun rays shining through the roof, looks like wood and cutouts for light. I wander around in the dim light, admiring the numerous large chairs. Ornate and unique, for each member of the council, I presume.

I hear a deep, bellowing voice speaking the foreign language, it almost scares me and I jump to turn around. "I'm sorry," my voice cracks, "Ah-hmn, I'm sorry, I don't understand your language."

"Very well," he says, as I look around for him, his voice resonates in the hall, making it hard to pinpoint. "What is your name?"

"I go by James," I reply, turning around to try to find him, "You must be King Borro."

"Mhm," it sounds like he's clearing his throat, "Yes." I turn around to see the largest, most ornate chair, and a figure steps out from behind.

At least 8 feet tall, a ring of horns like a crown upon his head. His complexion is blood red and fierce, cold yellow eyes; a wide, alien nose centers his face. He wears a white skirt, showing his beast-like legs. "I recognize you," I say, "We have a file on you-"

"Yes, I know," he sits down on his *throne*, "I believe you call me, *the Icon of Sin.*"

"I have documents I've been instructed to read to you to mediate diplomacy-"

"Why are you here?" he interrupts me.

"Diplomacy."

"Why are *you* here?" he persists.

I scratch my head in confusion, "I don't understand-"

"One of my subordinates informed me you have previous ties to one of our own; something quite unheard of, considering the extensive extermination your people carried out."

"We'd like a second chance at diplomacy-" he starts laughing, deep and thunderous. He finally stops and leans on his fist.

"Tell me," he continues, "Do *your* people really want diplomacy? Or do they want another resource to exploit."

"*I* want diplomacy," I state to him, "My superiors want peace; to them, this place is a treasure trove of new sciences- If I had my documents-"

"Very well," he stands back up, "I will assemble the council, Kiira will send for you."

With nothing else to do, I bow and walk back towards the door. It opens and I see Kiira standing there with her eye-patch. She leads me back out in the suns where everyone was waiting for me.

"How'd it go?" Henry asks me, "Scary lady right here wouldn't even let us listen."

I look over to see Kiira's cold glare. "It went, *alright*."

Martta was right, when the suns are on the horizon, it turns a nice red color. It's not like the sunset on Earth, I'm starting to get used to it. "Damn, the air here is so damn crisp!" Trevor just supremely inhales and loudly lets it out. Some of the others just laugh.

"Some of the natives are gathering again to look at us," Rick says, "Should we do some target practice?" he makes a *PEW PEW* noise with finger guns.

"Not funny, Rick," Henry chastises him, but he laughs anyway.

The suns finally set, and it gets dim. The red sun has moved a quarter of the way across, getting pretty close to setting. I look at the watch and listen to the soothing ticking.

"We should at least do some exploring," Rick says, "I'm no cartographer, but I'd like to see something different than grass fields."

"It's grass for miles," Henry laughs, "Like Kansas."

I stand up from the ground and look for the haze of the anchors. I look the way we came and see the white glow leading off in the horizon. I look to Harru, whose nearly asleep leaning on his spear.

"Hey, Harru," I call out to him, but he ignores me.

"Anyways, James," Henry says to me, "How much longer is it going to take for them to bring us in again, it's been, like, 48 hours?"

"Borro said he's 'assembling the council'," I tell him, with air quotes.

"Dude, what'd he look like?" Trevor asks me, "You said he's filed under *the Icon of Sin.*"

"He was, at least, 8 feet tall," I say, "Blood red skin, looks like he wears a crown."

"Bruh, seriously?"

"Yeah, now to think of it, he didn't have wings." Harru smacks the back of my head. I turn around and he gives me a dirty look.

"Borro is king," he says, "*You're* not."

"Yeah, sorry," I tell him, as he goes off in his little spot.

"Harru?" I try to call out to him again, "How long has Borro been king?"

The whole group quiets down, and Henry shuffles through his bag for a recorder. But he just stares in silence. "I'm telling ya'," Rick says, "He doesn't speak that good of English." I look to see the anchor a couple of feet away, glowing white from charging in the sun.

Something zips past all of us sitting on the ground, but Harru doesn't seem concerned. Rick pulls out his pistol and starts waving it around.

The thing zips past us again, I catch a glimpse of a white fur-ball running past, it almost looked like a rabbit. *BANG!* I see a bright flash from Rick firing a shot into the ground and I hear the grass disturbed as it runs off.

Harru readies his spear, aiming at Rick. "Dammit, Rick!" I shout.

"What?!" he shouts back, "It could've been poisonous!"

"You can't just fire at every little thing!"

"It *could've* been poisonous!"

"Harru?" I stand up and turn to him, "Was that thing dangerous?"

"No," he says, "Not dangerous."

"See?!" I turn back around.

"How am *I* supposed to know that?"

"Just," I rub back my hand on my head, "Just, dammit Rick.

"Just; everyone calm down!" I try to say.

"Yo, James," Trevor walks up to me, "Imma go back to the portal and have them toss my ukulele through, I need some entertainment."

I see Kiira walking up to us in the distance, "Give it a minute, Trevor, let's have her come to us first."

She finally gets to us, brushing her hand through the tallgrass, exchanging some words with Harru. "James," she calls for me, "Some of the council have arrived; they're all very intrigued with you."

"That's good right?" I ask.

"They might want to eat you," she says with a very straight face.

"That's a joke right?" Henry asks, "Because that is a good way-"

I shush him, waving my hand. "Anyways, a few of my men need something from the access point," I point to Trevor, "Can you tell Harru to accompany them?"

She rolls her eyes, and says something to Harru with some hand movements, "The rest of you, follow me.

"Do you have your *documents*, James?"

I nod and we all start walking our two ways. I see the building come into view, with multiple, large palanquins sitting on regular intervals around the building. They seem to match the thrones on the inside. We all get closer and the palanquins are bigger than I first thought. I know Borro is 8 feet tall, but everyone else I've seen who isn't a hybrid aren't nearly as tall as that.

"Only James," she announces to everyone, "Bring your devices." she points to my guns.

"Kiira, they're called 'guns'."

"I don't like that word," she replies, opening the door. She calls into the building and another demon walks out, clad in leather and a spear. They exchange words and she motions to me. I pull my documents out of my bag and toss the bag to Henry.

The deep sounds of them talking to each other resonates in my chest. I see King Borro and 5 others; two females. "You've come back," Borro says to me.

I see nearly a full house, with more native demons standing guard with, assuming, their respective leaders. A few of them have what looks like bows and a quiver. One of the females looks at me, she's about 7 feet tall, sitting on the throne. Her horns are smooth ivory, pointing downwards and wrapping forward; it appears Borro is the only one without wings. She points and me, saying something and laughing.

I clear my voice and pull out my documents, but before I can start Kiira says something to me, "They want a demonstration of your weapon."

"I don't-" I clear my throat again and speak loudly, "I don't think that's a good idea."

"Why is that?" Borro asks.

"It's very loud, very bright," I reply, "Very violent."

The woman with the ivory horns says something like she's persisting. "*Prela* insists," Kiira translates.

"I don't-" I try to say

"She won't ask twice," Kiira whispers to me.

"Alrighty," I roll up the papers and put them under my arm. With my other hand, I pull out my pistol and aim toward the ground, "It's *very* loud," I tell Kiira, "Tell them to cover their ears."

She turns and presumably tells them. I see a few of them lean forward, but none of them cover their ears. *BANG!* The sound echoes in the room and leaves a lingering ring in my ears. I slide the pistol back into its holster and grab the papers again. They all start conversing amongst themselves.

"What are they saying?" I ask Kiira.

She leans over to me, "Prela is warring over the sea, and she's heard many things about your weapons."

"No, absolutely not," I say, "Under no circumstances am I giving guns to anybody here."

She announces something to them, and they start discording. Prela, I assume, starts shouting at me. "She's asking why bring them then?"

"For our protection," I tell her, "I've come to make peace, not war."

Borro claps his hands, echoing about and everyone shuts up. "Tell us what you have," he commands.

I clear my throat once more, "Yes.

"First order of business," Kiira starts translating, "A complete ceasefire between our two peoples-"

"*Our* peoples?" Borro interrupts me, "Do you think we're *one* people?"

"Uh," I pause, "I realize now, that there are multiple nations, but that hasn't come to light to my superiors."

"Ceasefire?" Kiira asks me to explain.

"Peace; uh, neither side attacks the other." Kiira starts to translate but multiple demons start bickering.

"You expect us to agree, after your *extermination*."

"That was then, this is now," I tell him, "That's exactly why I'm here."

I know he doesn't agree but everyone quiets down. I start reading the official statement from the president to them. Borro seems like the only one who's fully comprehending what I'm saying.

"And whose words are these?" Borro asks, with the council talking amongst themselves.

"The leader of *my* nation, he's an elected leader called the president," I tell him, "Another request from my leader is that you allow scientists into your borders to collect and trade information-"

The council starts again in discord, shouting at me and each other. Borro claps, and everything falls silent. "What do we get out of it?"

"We can give you recipes for better building materials; techniques to create stronger materials-"

"Such as?" he interrupts me, all the council members look right at me expecting me to say something. I take a moment to think about something that could convince them; concrete has been used to build large, strong structures, and it's something easily made. But they seem to be driven by war, or at least some of them.

Glass is useful, but it's not as enticing. "What do you know about your world's geography?" I ask Kiira.

"What do you mean?" she replies.

"Do you know what's beyond this place?" she looks at me confused, turning to me.

"If you go up between where the yellow suns sets and rises, you will reach mountains," she explains to me, pointing to the direction, "And in the opposite direction, there's a river where another village resides."

I turn back to Borro and the council, "Do you know what a map is, King Borro?" I ask.

"I'm familiar with the word," he says, "But I have yet to see one."

"We can bring in a cartographer and teach you how to make maps- it could revolutionize the way you travel and communicate," I tell them, and I can see in Borro's eyes he's interested, "And we could teach you to make boats to sail across the ocean."

Kiira starts translating, and they all go into awe and start conversing. "They're asking what's beyond the grand sea?"

I pull her to the side, "Do they not know the world is circular?" Her eyes instantly widen in shock and I can see the gears grinding in her head. "There's probably a whole other continent on the other side-"

"Stop, that's-" she turns back around. She starts talking to them. I hear shock and awe from all of them, except Borro. Prela starts shouting and pointing at the person next to her. Kiira turns back to me, "They don't believe you," she says.

"Tell them to accept and we'll prove it."

"Very well," Borro stops everyone by clapping once more, "I accept." he says something in his language, and one by one, all of them say something. Kiira whispers to me that they're either accepting or declining to peace and allowance in their borders.

The last one speaks and Kiira pulls on my arm, leading me back outside. I turn to see Trevor strumming on his instruments and a couple locals listening from the tallgrass.

I pull my bladder from the water extractor and start drinking from it. Kiira has been accompanying us in place of Harru for better communication, but she's come armed. The boys have been getting more leisurely, waiting patiently for bureaucracy to do it's thing with stone age peoples.

I got an order from the other side when Trevor got his instrument to start information collection via recordings. "So, Kiira," I turn on my recorder, and attaching it to my suit, "What have you been up to since you got back?"

"I went to war, and came back to be a war consultant," she tells me.

"Where's the war?"

She glares at me, wanting me to stop. I take the hint and turn off my recorder and look the other way. "So," I trail off, "Where's-"

"You don't want to know the answer to that question," she cuts me off.

"Anyways, I've been given orders to start collecting information now that Borro-"

"*King* Borro," she corrects me.

"*King* Borro has agreed to the requests, that we launch a drone to map out the area and the sky."

"Drone?"

"It's, uh, like a," I pause to think of something, "a *yousi*, it's a machine that flies."

She pauses to think, "Let me see it."

"Rick!" I call out, "Time to launch drone B-2!"

"Not A-1?" he shouts back, turning to say something to someone, probably badmouthing me. I whistle out to collect everyone and we all start following the anchors to find our way back. I look up to see some *yousi* flying in a v-formation up above. "What are these sticks?" she asks.

"They're anchors, they just allow us to find our way between two points."

"You know," Rick walks back to us, "You're kinda sexy-" Kiira thrusts her claws directly into his chest, sinking into the armor and splitting it in one direction.

Rick raise his hands and goes back to the front, "Kinda hot, but-"

We arrive at the portal and I look through the hole in the wall to see scientists working on the other side. Henry and I start pulling the large case of drones through the wall to the outside until it's in the clear.

I open the latches and we start lifting the one labeled 'B-2'. It's a surveillance drone equipped with a powerful computer and AI, fully powered by solar and can stay in this sky almost indefinitely. I open the case for the drone and pull out the body and we set it on the dirt. It's about as long as I am tall, but a third the weight.

"What's that?" Kiira kneels and points to the camera array, "And what does it do?"

"It's called a camera, sweetie," Rick butts in, "It's like your eyeball; it sees things and reports back to us."

"It's true," I say to try and diffuse, "It'll map out the landscape and collect other information."

"Fine, I'll allow it," she grudgingly says.

Henry and Trevor continue assembly and start attaching the wings. Not too long after, it's complete. I kneel down to it, and press my thumb on the fingerprint reader to turn it on. It starts whirring and the camera array starts to move, testing itself. Kiira takes a step back and readies her claws.

The light turns from red to blue to green, signally it's ready. "So we just let it take off on the path and it'll be good?" Trevor asks me.

"Basically." a few of us pick it up, and align it with the straight part of the path back to the village. A compartment opens up on the bottom, towards the back, and a blue glow starts coming out the back and the drone is on it's way into the sky. Kiira still looks suspicious, but that *is* her job.

Rick starts assembling the main computer with the solar panel attachment. Kiira starts calling out to someone, in a happy mood, which is a first for me. I turn to see some larger demons trudging through the tallgrass, probably 20 or 30 of them coming through in the distance. I hear them calling back and waving.

"Who are they?" I ask.

"Farmers, coming to bring us food," she replies.

"Computer's up," Rick says.

"They come every 4 weeks to bring us a harvest," she explains, as I struggle to turn on my recorder, "They travel from village to village bringing food."

I finally get the recorder on, "*Subject Kiira has informed me that food source and farmers collect themselves away from villages and they frequent the villages with rations every 4 local weeks.*

"Kiira, how many days are in your weeks?" I ask, but she disregards me, staring me down with her one angry eye.

"It turns me on to see angry wom-" Rick tries to say, before being shut up by Henry,

"Why didn't you come alone?" She asks, presumably to herself, "King Borro is only interested in you."

"My superiors deemed it necessary to supervise me," I reply.

After a couple days of watchful supervision by Kiira, Harru comes running down the path that's become blazed into the tallgrass. He stops just shy of Kiira and they exchange some words and Kiira turns back around and tries to open her mouth, but raises her finger and just waits.

She clears her throat and says, "King Borro has summoned all of you."

"Wow," Rick says, nudging one of the others, talking like an idiot.

Kiira quickly grabs me and pulls me aside, but the words in her mouth fail to come out. She just raises her finger again and prepares herself, "You know what? I'll just leave it as a surprise."

We start the trek back into the village. "Why did he summon all of us?" I ask. Kiira and Harru exchange some more words.

"He doesn't seem to trust all of you," she replies.

"I mean-"

"He also needs to told about your *drone*," she starts, "Soldiers have returned from the war, and the council is planning another attack beyond the sea." she goes off mumbling to herself. Harru looks pretty agitated also.

We arrive to see a few more of the palanquins missing, with one of the council members getting into theirs and a few demons lifting it off the ground. We get to the front and see four hybrid demons standing guard with spears and bows.

They do something I can only guess to be a salute to Kiira, and she just opens the door and we all funnel in. The main chamber is empty, given a few natives standing at each throne. "Follow me," she says, leading us through another door into an equally large room.

Everyone inside turns to look at us and fall silent. They I surround a table with extremely crude carvings and stone scattered on there. King Borro sits at the head of the table. Kiira does the salute thing and they return the action.

"Welcome," King Borro greets us, eyeing each one of us, "The generals have returned and I wanted to know what you think."

We walk up to a space at the table. Someone starts talking to Kiira, and she starts explaining the whole thing. She says the main portion is the grand sea, and the stones were the two sides' troops and she gives me a run down of the battle that took place.

"Tell me, *humans,*" Borro says, "What should we do next?"

"I- I'm not a strategist-" I say, but Rick just shoves past me.

"Do they have wings, like everyone here?" he asks, and Borro looks confused.

"Yes, they do," he replies, leaning on his fist.

"Is there land to either side of this lake?" he asks, "You can attack from either side instead of across." Kiira translates, and everyone starts murmuring.

"The sea separates the two lands, it's not known if there's land on either side," she replies.

"What about attacks from above?"

"It's too difficult to get that high," one of the hybrids tells him.

I pull Rick back and shove him a little, "What are you doing?"

"*Trading information,*" he says sarcastically.

"We're here to establish peace-"

"And the sooner their war is over-" he chuckles, "How do you even know this is the right side?

"We're only here because of a quantum fluke."

"I'm ordering you to stop-"

"You can't order me around dipshit," he shoves me back, going back to the table, "We're not on Earth, and they'll never know." he goes back to strategizing with the generals. I take a few steps back to think.

"Is it really that bad that he's helping them?"

"He's a guerrilla, Henry." I turn to look at him, "It's not healthy." he shrugs it off.

Kiira rushes to the door, and I hear some shouting on the other side. The door kicks open and I see Kiira trying to keep someone at bay.

"Calm down!" Kiira shouts, and I witness Martta kick her to the floor. She comes into view and the first thing I see are the two asymmetrical gazelle-like horns.

"You!" Martta screams. She snatches a spear from a guard and chucks it at me. I dodge just in time as it flies past my ear. She screams again and steals another spear and throws it again, but it bounces off my armor.

"You!" she gets frustrated and screams again, grabbing a bow and firing an arrow. It soars through the air and digs right into my chest piece. screeching, she runs after me, but stops just shy of tearing my throat out.

"That's enough," Borro announces. Rick starts laughing and I fall down, losing my balance. I can see the fury in her eyes, looming over me.

She finally goes away and walks up to Rick, "You're in my spot."

He laughs a little, "I'm not looking for a fight." he raises his hands and moves to the side.

"Why are *they* even here?!" she grits through her teeth, "I wasn't even told that *they* arrived."

"I've allowed them to stay in promise that they show me a *map*."

"A map?" she whispers. I see her hand scratching the tables, creating wooden curls in the wake. "A map, Borro?"

"They bring promises-'

"Empty promises," she interrupts him.

"Actually, the drone should beam us it's map data when the sun sets-" Martta snatches another spear and throws it at Rick, landing in his cracked armor. He gets pushed back and backs up to the wall.

"Alright, bitch," Rick pulls out his pistol, but I jump in front of it before he thinks of firing. "Y'know *James*, I wouldn't mind shooting you too."

I look around to see nearly everybody armed and ready except Borro, who's just sitting there, watching what will happen. "Put the gun away."

"Fine! But I won't like it," he waves it around, before putting it back in its place.

"You're all excused," Borro says to us, "Kiira will lead you out."

"James!" Trevor calls out, "Data's back." I look up to see the drone in the sky, flying past us up above. Trevor opens the screen to the receiver. We all gather behind him as he scrolls around the map, zooming out.

"I guess that's why we never see them fly," Henry remarks at the plateau we're atop of, "Air's too thin up this high for their size."

"There," Rick says, "There's the lake; what elevation is that?" Trevor switches the modes, and I see a sharp drop off before the lake. "Image that area next."

"I'm the one giving orders, Rick," I remind him.

"We have to image it eventually, James, why not now?" Trevor starts typing in the commands and slams the 'Enter' key.

"I've never seen anything like it," I hear a woman's voice.

"Geez!" Rick gets scared and flings out his gun, but I think quick and move it upwards before it fires. *BANG!* The gun goes off and leaves a ringing in my ear.

I look over to see Kiira looking over our shoulder to the display. "Is that the map?"

"It's a picture of the landscape with some crude altitude data," I tell her, "Once enough data is collected, we'll beam it and have it printed out."

"The warriors go back out in a few days," she informs us.

"Convenient," Rick says, "the drone will be back in a few days."

I pull Kiira aside, far enough away where the boys won't hear us. "What happened to-"

"She went to war, Ost-," she catches herself, "*James*. It changed her; she went from being a spy to killing her own kind."

"But why is she so angry at me?"

"I don't know," she tells me, "She shuts me out too."

"Good, good," I tap her on the shoulder and walk back away.

Kiira leads us in the building into the war room. Rick just waltzes with a large tube and sets it on the table, pushing past someone. He unclips the roll and the map spreads out over the entire table. The demons at the table are in awe, making noises. I pick out Martta with her uneven horns, but she looks unimpressed.

"Behold, Borro," he announces, "A map!"

"Incredible," Borro says, "It's like, the eyes of a great *goso*."

"What- what is this material called? It's incredible." Borro leans over and feels the map."

"It's called paper, it's made from wood, like this table."

"The secrets you hold," he whispers to himself.

"There!" someone says, followed by the discords of people shouting at landmarks, looking at the encompassing land surrounding the lake at the base of the plateau, looking at the villages on the other side of the lake. They point at strategize on what to do next, thinking of their next attack.

Borro claps and everything falls silent. I look at him, seeing him think. Rick backs away, leaving them to their devices; Borro is completely on board with our agreement, and he can convince the council.

"We'll leave you to your map, King Borro," I pull Rick from the crowd.

"What are you doing, it's just getting good?" he argues, pushing me back.

"You helping them in their war council *isn't* part of our treaty," I tell him.

"It's working, ain't it?" he shoves me, and I shove him back. Henry comes and breaks us up. Rick shows me the bird and walks out of the war room. Trevor and another walk out with him.

I look around and fail to find Martta standing at the table, but I approach anyway. "Hopefully, this solidifies our agreement between our two societies, and we hope we can continue furthering ourselves."

"Yes," Borro says, "This *is* magnificent."

I pull along everyone else in our caravan out of the war room. The door opens and I see Martta slug Rick in the face, forcing him to the ground. Trevor's also on the floor, holding his face.

"You little-" Rick tries to say before being kicked in the crotch, followed by Rick cursing.

She takes a breath and moves her hair out of her face. "As much as I take joy that Rick just got kicked in the nuts," I say to her, "What are you doing?"

"Taking out some," she pauses, "frustration."

"There's a thing called therapy-"

"I don't want to hear it!" she screams. She opens and closes her hand, probably to relieve some pain, but I notice something odd: her nails have been trimmed down. "I waited for you! And waited!"

"It took time-"

"I don't want to hear it!" she pulls on her hair and screams. Kiira comes bursting through the door, being followed Borro with both hands behind his back; a second, seeing him walking.

Rick crawls back up on his feet on his weary legs, holding his groin. "What happened here?" Borro asks.

"Don't even get me started," Martta grits. She starts rushing up to me, probably ready to strike. *BANG!* The sound echoes in the hall. Martta stops and puts her hand over her chest, seemingly scratching it.

Blood starts leaking from her hand. "Dammit, I missed- I mean, these things have hearts right?" Rick boasts, "Start exec. triple-six."

Somebody throws a spear at him, but it bounces off the armor. An arrow flies through the air but misses. I pull out my gun, but *BANG!* It gets knocked from my hand, along with a finger.

"Rick!" *BANG!* Someone fires another bullet and Martta falls to the ground. *BANG!* Another body falls. *BANG!* Something bites me through my chest.

"We all know your little secret, *Ostin!*" he shouts, firing another bullet into my leg, bringing me to my knees. "Dammit, I swear this thing is off, give me yours."

He trades guns with Trevor and walks up to me. "Rick-" I try to say, losing blood fast.

"It is Dedrick!" he shouts, waving his weapon around, "Dedrick Panzer!

"Can't sell guns if there's no war!" he laughs. *BANG! BANG!* He keeps firing into Martta's body, but she's stopped flinching. He turns to me as I crawl to her, seeing Borro leaning, dying on the wall. "That's exactly what I'm starting."

"I hate you, Ostin; I hate-" My vision goes out as does my hearing. Ringing is the only thing left I hear left, muffled gunshots in the background.

The Eye Within

I feel something watching me. I open my eyes from my slumber, and see the darkness in the dead of night; is it a beast staring back at me?

No. It's but a chair with a coat from the yester day.

I take my steps, ready to face the infant corpse in the bathtub. My reality is shaken with the creaks in the floorboards; *shaky shaky* goes my head in the darkness with no real point of reference.

Yet there is no fetus awaiting me beyond the door, but a mirror me staring back at me. The demented demon smile with an eye single to the despair in my heart. The light flips on, revealing nothing but my naked body awaken from my bed.

The light goes away and the demon returns, so I turn away and return to the kitchen where water awaits my lips. Every step down feels like an eternity of being chased by the nightmares in my mind. *Creak creak* goes the eyes beneath my feet as I drive my feet into the pupils of my inner mind.

The water touches my lips, and my eyes close for a brief moment and I witness the horrors of my dreams once more: the corpse in the bathtub and the flashing of the Gatling.

0-0-1 The Gate Guardian

Destruction of The Axis

RING! RING! RING! The cashier keeps ringing the bell for an order of food that's *currently* being made. "Charles! Get the food out!"

"I'm working as fast as the chef, Myrtle!" I shout back, loading up yet another plate of food, and running off back to the tables.

"Here you go," I say, laying down a sandwich and grits and swiftly moving on to the next table, "And there you go."

"Charlie!" I hear Myrtle shouting at me again.

I set down the last plate, "Have a nice meal-" I rush back to behind the counter and pick up the large special from Ugly Myrtle and some fat customer has been on my case about.

"Sorry for the wait-"

"Can it, lady," he interrupts me, "Just give me my food and get out of here, bitch."

"*Okay*," I reply, "Have a nice meal."

"Charles," Ugly Myrtle says, "That's the third one today, you need to step up your game."

"Okay, Myrtle," I say back, grabbing another plate and busing out to the table.

I stop midstep to look at one of the televisions on a news station. I look around and realize a majority of the customers are glued to the intellavision, with only the smaller kids with their eyes covered by their mothers.

"The Red Army is progressing further across the continent, veering northward towards the Anglin Empire despite current military sources saying that the Red Army had no interest in-"

"That's enough of that," I say, turning the intellavision to a cartoon channel, and continue to buss tables.

"Charles!" she shouts across the restaurant.

"Yes, Myrtle?" I yell back.

"Quit messing with the IV!"

"I'm just-" I shout, "Nevermind."

I put my hands behind my back and pull the strings to my corset uniform for the restaurant as I walk down the street. I look around, trying to enjoy the nice weather before I go in for my 10-hour shift.

I walk up to the restaurant and pull on the locked door. "Freaking Myrtle," I say to myself, looking through the darkened window to find no one in there.

I back away a little bit and see the reflection behind me and see a silver man, towering above the city. "What the?" I whisper to myself, turning around to see the giant silver man pushing over Freelong Tower in downtown.

I hurry to get my keys from my purse, hurrying my little fingers through the trinkets. "Frick, frick, frick," I say, realizing they were left on my side table. I zip up my bag and look around, watching the tallest tower in the city fall down to the ground. I see a shock wave full of dirt and dust start moving outward.

I hear the rumble of tanks turn the corner on the street. I look over my shoulder to see big vehicles marching towards me. "Evacuate! Evacuate!" I hear a man shout, brandishing the red army uniform. I start running away from them and one of my heels breaks off, throwing me to the ground.

I hear footsteps run towards me as I try to get back up. Someone lifts me up. "Let me go!" I yell, trying to punch my way out of his hold.

"This is a full state evacuation," he says, "0-0-1 has lost control and-" a huge energy ray aimed right at my restaurant. The place explodes and I feel the intense heat from the ray moving down the street. I start screaming in calamity as the soldier carries me off. He tosses me into a truck where another man pulls me down after another explosion.

"Go! Go! Go!" someone shouts as the truck starts turning back around in the street. I finally lift my head up to see the death ray blasting away my neighborhood.

"Oh-" I start crying before I'm grabbed and shoved into a seat.

"Stay down!" he shouts over the destruction, "Didn't you get the evacuation demand? It was broadcast statewide!"

"I didn't-" I try to say.

"Move out!" he shouts, "0-0-1 has lost control!"

The truck starts to turn around and I see the war tanks marching forward further into the city, but we're driving into the enemy's side.

"Where are you taking-" I try to ask before getting cut off by an explosion.

"We're taking you to safety, behind 0-0-1," he says, covering his head from debris. Once it clears, he slaps a pair of handcuffs around my wrists. The engines of the truck roars and we speed up and I see even more destruction.

I look up to the sky as we drive deeper into the city and see overseas' planes flying overhead, raining fire down on the giant silver man, but I see it swat the planes out of the air.

And then I see it: the big plane, the kind that drops the city-erasing bombs. I see it drop a small spec from the underside. I raise my arms over my head and... *FLASH!*

I feel the cold touch against all my body, then an intense burning sensation eating away at my hair and skin, only sparing the areas covered by my arms. I hear the Red Army men shouting and the car swerves and jumps up as we hit something. The rumble and the shock wave hit and the glass shatters all around.

I look back up, feeling the crunching of my sintered skin and arm hair. To see the fireball seemingly frozen in time with the silver man reaching into it. The longer I stare at it, the darker it becomes, the fireball turning almost black in the air.

"What the hell is that?" I shout, pointing at the silver man.

"Get down!" a soldier pushes my arm back and standing over me. Bombs start going off and chaos begins to ensue. I hear the radio on his chest start chattering.

"0-0-1 just absorbed the nuclear blast and seemingly went docile!" the radio says, but then the death ray from the silver man blasts into the air and strikes the big plane.

"Not docile!" he says back into the radio, "*Not* docile!"

I look up again at the horrors and I see the blank face of the silver man staring right at me, it seems. And the ray hits right next to the truck, tossing the truck to and fro. "Not *fracking* docile!" he shouts, signaling something to someone, "Haul ass, man!"

The car screeches and starts moving erratically before stabilizing. I look around and try to lift my arm, but I'm still cuffed down.

"Where-" I try to say, interrupted by some gunfire, "Where are you taking me?!" We pass by some more tanks marching through the city and I see all the destruction that's been wrought by the Red Army.

"Somewhere safer than this!" he shouts back, being followed by another explosion.

"So, young lady," someone walks in this room I've been put in. They drove me all the way to the coast where I saw, like footsteps in the snow, the annihilation of two cities. They lead me into a boat and pulled me along while I was in utter shock. "Here's some good news: you're out of harm's way-"

"Out of harm's way?" I retort, "What the hell was that silver man?"

"That, miss," he says, "Is classified information on both sides of this war."

"*That's classified*," I mock him.

"You're out of harm's way," he continues, "But you're also technically a war prisoner now."

"What?!" I express my surprise, "I'm not- I'm a- a waitress at- at the Betty's"

"Not anymore, 0-0-1 laid waste to your entire city. Thankfully, it seems that everyone *but you* got the evacuation demand," he brushes back his hair, "Why is that by the way, it was on intellavision for, like, 6 hours; the radio is still going on."

"I don't have one, it's too expensive, and- and who listens to the radio anymore."

"Anyway," he tries to say something else, "You're with the Red Army now, and you'll be placed overseas in our territory."

"Isn't the Anglin Empire your territory now, can't I just go home?"

"Your *entire* city was destroyed, remember," he reminds me, "You no longer have a home." I try to stand up, but the chain snaps on the cuffs. He tosses me a plastic bag full of something, "It's applesauce, to tide you over."

He walks over and flips on an intellavision and promptly walks out. I look down at my arm with some emergency burn patches and think to myself, *What the hell am I into now.*

The intellavision finally tunes in to some war propaganda channel from the Red Army. Trumpets and video of armies marching in unison. "Do your part in the war! Get a job, work hard, buy bonds!"

My stomach grumbles and it's going to be a long day.

One of the more good looking soldiers pulls on my cuff's chain through this crowd of people. "Come on," he pulls, "Charlie, was it? How are your burns?" I walk along in silence in this huge group of people, I think they're all immigrants moving inland. I keep hearing the same trumpet tune from the war propaganda played on repeat.

I look up above all the people and see 10 or so check-in stations that everyone is funneling through. Soldiers with guns standing in between each one and one more checking everyone in.

"Is everyone in the Red Army?" I retort.

"Every able-bodied young man between 17 and 40; the second-largest military in the world," he replies, "For me, though- you're probably thinking 'do I really know who I'm fighting for?' For me, it's economic stability. I got little siblings, y'know."

"What a sob story-"

"No, Charlie," he says, "These people right here next to you; they got sob stories. *You* got a sob story."

"Hail Hister, right?" I mock him.

"Hey, do yourself a favor and watch what you say around here," he tells me, "Captain pulled a lot of strings just to put you here, he's got a soft spot, y'know, but they got ears on every inch of this country."

"Where am I, really?" I ask him.

"Lordov Check-in, northern Yekiv province," he replies.

"That's the-" some lady bumps right into my burns in my arm, "That's the first straight answer I've gotten this past week."

"We're almost at the checkpoint," he turns to me, "I cannot stress this enough, after that checkpoint, Charlie, you are a citizen of this great country and you must abide by its laws or so help you."

"*So help me-*" I mock him, but he pull me close and whispers into my ear.

"Keep that up, and you're going to end up in a concentration camp," he whispers. My spine shivers and my arm begins to hurt, "You'll be a pretty face once you've healed up."

He pulls me up to the check-in and the armed soldier looks at me and shakes his head in shock. "What the hell happened to her?"

"Pull her out of Greenwich," he replies, handing him my chain.

"No shit, huh," he says, "Come here pretty lady, let's check you in

"Name."

"Ch-charlie," I clear my throat.

"Charlie what?" the check-in soldier asks.

"Wertson."

"Occupation?"

The handsome soldier walks up, "Um, she's, uh, war prisoner. There should be some special paperwork for that."

"You should've led with that," he looks over the desk at his name badge, "Charles."

I look over to see him pulling out a file cabinet and looking through stacks of paper. Finally, he pulls out a form and begins to write on it. "Charlie Wertson, was it?" he asks.

"Yes-"

"Yes," *Charles* interrupts me. I turn my head and scowl at him for interrupting me.

"Where'd you pick up this broad, Charles?" another soldier asks.

"Greenwich," he says. The man behind the desk looks at him in disbelief.

"Greenwich was wiped off the map after a full state evacuation. There should've been no one on the island."

"Just do the paperwork," Charles looks over the desk, "*Yokov.*"

The soldier behind the desk continues to ask me my age and whatnot until the paper is full. He runs it through a machine and it spits out an exact replica of the paperwork, something I haven't seen too often.

He stamps and hands me the copy and says, "Congratulations, you are not a beloved citizen of the New Staten Empire. Please proceed forward and take your introduction manual."

Charles pulls me along beyond the threshold and grabs the 5-centimeter thick book for me.

"I cannot stress this enough Charlie," he goes on again, unlocking my cuffs and setting me free, "Read this book, and abide by the rules here."

"I've seen the camps on the intellavision," I retort, "How can I?"

"Because you have no choice here," he replies, pushing the textbook in my burnt hand. He pulls out a small slip of paper and puts it in my other hand, "If you need anything, I'll be back in town in 3 weeks."

BOOM! The ground shakes and some dust falls down on me. *Not again*, I think to myself. *BOOM!* People start screaming and running about. I shield myself from the dust falling. The hum of planes passes by above as I look up to see them: the Allies overhead.

"Go that way!" Charles points deeper into the facility as he brandishes a pistol.

"Wait!" I call out, but he runs off. I look around and *BOOM!* Another explosion goes off, forcing me to run further and further into the Lordov Checkpoint.

I hear turrets going off outside, followed by explosions. The remaining soldiers herd everyone together, shouting in another language.

"Bunker! Bunker!" Someone shouts, pointing to a pair of huge double doors, slowly opening by themselves. Push comes to shove to get inside, people just barreling through each other. Someone rams right into my patched burns, pushing me over in agony.

"Go! Go! Go!" Soldiers shout. Another bomb goes off and I see part of the building collapsing, spewing dust and rubble everywhere, with a piece hitting my head.

I try to lift my head back up, my vision blurry, and try and find a way into the bunker. I stumble onto my feet, but I'm pushed over by another bystander. Everything seems to be muffled, but I can still hear the turrets firing off.

Someone pulls me up, but I can't see who it is. They carry me through the crowd until we make it through the double doors and I'm blinded by fluorescent white light. I push them away and get on my feet while my vision clears up.

"Wha-what's happening?" I manage to say.

"The Allies are bombing the Checkpoint," I hear Charles say.

"I thought you left," I stabilize on my feet.

"Captain put you in my care," he says, my eyes focusing on a rifle he's holding, "You're my top priority, that is after God and country."

"Ha. Ha," I sarcastically laugh at him.

He announces something in another language to the hoard of people in the bunker, waving his hands at everyone.

"I think the raid is done!" he repeats.

I fall on my behind and try to curl up, thinking, *What the hell is happening? A week ago I was working 10-hour shifts at Betty's.*

Charles picks me up by the arm, "This isn't the time to cry."

BOOM! Dust falls from the ceiling. I look around to see people huddling around each other, whimpering like dogs. Charles' radio starts talking and he talks back. "They're gone!" he shouts as the bunker doors roll open.

My eyes poke through to see the carnage left behind, the roof over the entrance area completely caved in, rubble everywhere. I clutch the paperwork tighter, folding it up and sliding it into my pocket.

"Hold on to that," he whispers into my ear, "Single file! Single File!"

I begin to notice the beating drum that is my heart in my ear. I look down at my hands to see them shaking, but I subside the thoughts and walk out of the bunker.

"My mother is very hospitable, you can stay with my family until the government programs kick in," Charles says. He looks at the taxi driver and gives him the instructions to the destination.

"How-How often exactly do bombings happen, again?" I ask.

"That girl needs to watch her mouth there, soldier," the driver says.

"She hasn't read the citizen's handbook yet," he replies before leaning to me, "The Amerians bomb our territories almost weekly, they're unrelenting."

"What about France?" I retort.

"Watch her tongue, soldier!" the taximan shouts.

"Please, Charlie, refrain-"

"Refrain from what?!" I shout, "Am I just supposed to roll over and become a Nazi?"

The taxi slams to a stop, "Soldier, you need-"

"Don't make me arrest you," Charles snaps at him, "Drive!"

The car picks back up again, this time with the driver watching the road. "It's not so bad here, Charlie," he says, "It's nice here, it's economically stable, there are jobs; the Amerians won't fly out this far into the country.

"Look, if you like, I can even get a job like your old one; you're a waitress, right?"

"I'm not too eager to start busing tables again," I reply.

"We're here," the driver tells us.

I open the door and see an apartment complex; it looks new, nicely painted a shade of brown. He puts his hand on my back, leading me up the steps. "They're up on the second floor," he says, walking up the metal staircase.

He counts the doors and settles on one of them, and starts banging on the door. "Mama!" he yells, "Mama!"

The door unlocks, and I hear three locks slide and the door opens. A middle-aged woman answers and greets him in the other language. The converse and kiss each other on the cheeks.

"Mama," he says, "I need her to stay here while the government kicks in."

She replies in that other language and huddles me inside. It's nice, I see a couch and an intellavision, two more than I had back home. But that's all gone now, even my savings. I look over and see a young girl and a teenager sitting at a table. The table's nice too, it's made of glass.

"Did Charles bring home a wife this time?" the teenage girl asks the lady, but she doesn't reply in Anglish. The two girls laugh a little and the lady brings me a bowl of soup.

She repeats a word, and the teenager tells me, "She says to eat.

"Charles!," she shouts as he walks in behind me, "Who's this? She looks Amerian!"

"She's Anglin actually, Jessica. Treat her nicely," he replies, "It's lovely to see you too, but unfortunately, I can't stay. I have to go back out; can't stay for long."

"Can you bring me a gift next time?" *Jessica* asks.

"The Anglin island may not be around for much longer, but I'll try as hard as I can."

The lady forces the bowl into my hand and pulls me along to the glass table. "Wait, Charles!" I call out as I'm dragged by this lady.

"I'll be back in a couple of weeks!" he sarcastically waves goodbye as the door closes.

Jessica laughs, "So what's your story? Charles has had people stay here before; he's sentimental like that."

The lady sits me down at the table and hands me a spoon. "You should eat, it's pretty good. My mom's a good cook," she says.

"I'm, uh, from," I pause, circling the spoon, "Greenwich."

"Oh, no shit, huh?" she retorts, with her mother smacking the back of her head, "Sorry, ma."

The little girl repeats after her sister and is also promptly smacked by her mother. "I thought that place had a full-state evac?"

"I don't- didn't have IV or radio," I say, "I'd rather not talk about it, because I'm now apparently now a-"

"You sure don't anymore-" her mother smacks her again followed by some chatter, "You're right, that's insensitive." I lift the spoon, and take a sip on the soup; it's savory and still warm.

"What's your name?" the little girl asks.

"My name's, uh, Charlie," I reply, eating some more of the soup. I haven't had food this good in a while.

The lady, I think, talks to me but I don't understand. "She's asking if you have your paperwork, she'll take you to the office tomorrow to get it processed."

"Oh, that's okay-"

"She's insisting," she says, "The sooner, the better."

"I guess you can't say no then," I say, eating some more soup.

"So you're basically a war prisoner, right?" Jessica persists on private details, but her mother just smacks her, "Mama!"

"Why are you covered in bandages?" the little girl asks me, but their mother shuts her down.

"She says to eat, it's almost time for her favorite show, and then curfew," Jessica tells me. I circle the spoon in the soup, thinking about all this, but not going anywhere. Their intellavision flips on, and some propaganda that I've heard at least 20 times by now turns on.

Do your part, it says; *Buy bonds*, it says; And *Heil Hister*, it says, before it cuts to some silent film comedy. Everything's not in Anglish here, not even on the IV. The program goes on for an hour as we all watch from the table. Eventually, I do finish the soup and the lady takes it from me and begins to wash it.

BOOM! People start screaming about the restaurant, the ceiling cracks. I rush up to the window and see the silver man, blasting away with his ray of destruction. Beaming back of forth, destroying everything in sight.

"Charles!" Myrtle yells at me, "What the hell is going on!?"

"Myrtle!" I shout, "Everyone! Stay calm-"

The beam of death hits the west side of Betty's. I look to see in slow motion, the patrons being dissolved from the skin to the bone right before my eyes. I scream, freeze; everybody starts running around, pushing and shoving to get out.

Then the silver man looks at me, and I feel his deathly gaze shivering up and down my spine. I stare back at him like a deer stares into a car's headlights.

I come back to reality and realize it was a dream, but I'm hyperventilating, looking around this unfamiliar house. The sound of blood rushing through my ears is deafening, but I try to slow my breathing down.

"Everything's fine," I say to myself, "Every-everything is okay; where am I?

"I'm at-I'm at, uh," I look around, seeing the couch I'm on, the intellavision, "I'm at, uh, Charles'." My eyes adjust to the moonlit living room of this apartment.

"Oh, and I'm a Nazi," I tell myself as my breathing slows back down to normal giving me back my gift of sarcasm, "That's right."

"Yeah, you're *totally* a Nazi," I hear someone say, scaring me out of my wits, "Charles sometimes has bad dreams, too, y'know."

I recatch my breath, look to find Jessica, "I'm sure he's seen some shit."

"Careful to not let my mom hear you talk like that," she says, "She'll slap anyone."

We both chuckle a little. "What time is it?" I ask, rubbing my eyes.

"It's about an hour before sunrise," she replies, "5 in the morning."

"What are you doing up?"

I stand from the couch and start folding the blanket, and Jessica walks over to the kitchen. "I have trouble sleeping, that's all," she tells me, "You want some water?" She opens the cabinet and starts filling her glass from the faucet.

"Yeah, that'd be nice," I reply, walking over to their dining table, "it's nice here."

"Yeah, you could say that," she hands me a glass. I hear their mother start yelling from her room. The door opens and I see her ready for something.

"Mama!" Jessica shouts back. I awkwardly take a few steps back towards the couch as they talk to each other. "She's asking if your ready, the offices are opening soon," she tells me, followed by some more foreign yelling.

"Um," I pause, rubbing my face, "Yeah, I'm ready."

"Mardi!" Jessica shouts, for her sister I'm presuming, then making some exchanges with their mother. The little girl comes waddling out of her room.

Their mother walks over to me grabs my arm, pulling me along out the door. I look around to see no nightlife as the sun begins to peek through the mountainous horizon. Their mother starts chattering. "She says we're walking, it's only 10 minutes," Jessica translates.

As we walk down the street, the sun rises, shining on the clouds. I think to myself, *I haven't seen a sunrise like this in years*. But we walk and walk, turning a few corners into town, and it took much longer than 10 minutes. Finally, we walk up, what I think is, a post office, plastered with even more propaganda.

We go inside, and I hear nothing I can understand, but Jessica's mother pulls me along and starts talking with the guy at the counter.

"He needs your paperwork, did you bring it?" Jessica asks me.

"Um," I start patting down myself, but I find the papers in my front pocket, "Yeah, they're right here." I pull them out and hand them to the man.

He unfolds them and starts looking them over. He gets a look on his face and says something. "He says he hasn't seen this kind of paperwork, but he'll mail it out anyways," she translates, "But he'll just need a signature."

I walk up and look around the paper he has there, not being able to read any of it, "I, uh-"

The man writes an X on a few lines and motions me to take the pen. "I can help you," Jessica walks up and starts reading the page.

"I'm so glad people here are bilingual," I say. Jessica goes through the page, asking me the questions and filling it out for me. After a few minutes, it's all filled out and the man stamps it with a government seal.

"Now he just needs postage, and, uh," she pauses to listen to him, "They usually process this stuff in a week or so."

"I don't have any money," I confess, but their mother just pulls out her purse and rummages for a couple of coins to pay the postage. "Oh, uh, thanks," I say, with Jessica repeating it for me.

"Charlie!" Jessica shouts from the outside. I hear her footsteps up the iron stairs.

"Um," I clear my throat, not wanting to shout, "Yes?"

"You have a parcel!" she says, coming through the door, "It's from the government."

She hands it to me and it's all in another language. "What's it say?"

"It looks like, uh," she pauses to read the information stapled to it, "*Job* stuff. You should open it, see what it is."

I tear open the paper and I see a Jermain to Anglish dictionary and Jessica tells me there's a work uniform inside as well, from the note that was inside.

"On the 1st, Charlie," She tells me, "Don't be late." she raises her hands and wiggles her fingers at me to tease. "You'll be working for the government as a typist, like a *real* Nazi."

"Ha, ha," I slow laugh, "Very funny Jessica." I sigh, in a whirlwind of emotions, I contemplate this whole new life. My dreams are getting worse when I have them. I look at this tightly-folded ugly, military-green uniform that's 10 years out of style.

"Hey," she comes closer, purposely bumping into my shoulder, "Cheer up, at least you're not in Greenwich."

"I mean, it's not that this is technically better, but-" I pause, "I wish I was-"

"There were confirmed 0 casualties," She comforts me, "*Zero*."

I pull up the uniform top and take an extended look at it. It looks a little small for me, and there's a colored patch on the shoulder with a name tag, what I'm presuming to be, my name in Jermain.

"Don't worry," she says grabbing the bottom fringe on the fabric, "It stretches."

I keep walking up these ridiculously missized steps to this fantastically large military building. It's head and shoulders above the buildings next to it, branded with bright red and black swastikas and SS banners. And these steps are just too large for a single step, but too small for 2 steps.

My ankle rolls in these heels that Charles' mother allowed me to borrow, but I keep walking without falling. I look around to make sure no one saw me stumble, but I look to find beyond the glass doors are more than a few soldiers in red armbands hailing at each other, and walking away.

"Ah crap," I say to myself, "I forgot about that."

I lift up my skirt so I can walk a little faster up the steps, preparing myself for the impropriety I'm about to perform. I come to the door, and one of them opens the tinted glass door.

"Oh, uh, thank you," I say, "Um-"

"Hail Hister!" he announces, raising his arm.

"Oh, uh, right," I began to raise my arm, drop it, raise it again, "Hail, uh, *Hister?*"

He lowers his hand and motions for me to come over. "With conviction next time!" I hear an older, accented man shout, "You are graced with being in the motherland, darling! Now shout it!"

"Oh, uh," I stammer, clearing my throat, "Hail! Uh, *Hister.*"

"Conviction!" he shouts, marching over to me with his arm pointed up.

"Look, I'd rather not-"

"I know you're not from around here, Charlie," he taps my name tag with his finger, "Where are you from, darling?"

"I'm-I'm from Greenwich-"

"Oh, really?" he raises his voice, "A survivor!" he takes my arm and straightens it out above my shoulder. "Now, announce!"

I clear my throat, "Hail, Hister!" I quickly lower my voice, conscious I said it too loud.

"Perfect," he says, patting my shoulder, "Now where are you headed today?"

"I'm, actually, um, here for work."

"Ah, as a typist?" he says, tapping his finger on the colored badge, "Let me walk you to."

He motions me along and we begin to walk down into a hall. It's covered in 'military honor'; maps, portraits, photos, the like. The man is clad in the same ugly, military green, decorated with badges.

"Here we are," he opens a door, revealing a room with 5 by 5 grid of desks and chairs, filled with typewriters, women in uniforms and hats, and huge piles of paper, with an empty desk just for me. In uneasy unison, they all turn and smile at me. "*Guten tag*, my darling," he whispers into my ear, "That's what we say here."

"Yes," I clear my throat, "*Gu-guten tag*, everyone."

They all go back to their work, clacking away on the machines, dinging away on the bells, and then the door closes behind me. I freeze, just standing there with no intent when a woman with bright red hair walks up to me from behind a file cabinet.

"Guten tag," she says, before talking in Jermain.

"I-I, uh, don't speak Jermain," I tell her; she stops and calls out to someone.

One of the girls stands up to face us. "She says good morning. And she says you need to copy text from one paper to another with the machine, and set it aside. And it's all classified information. Understand?" she repeats.

"Yes, I under-" I clear my throat again, "I understand."

"Good," the redheaded lady says in a heavy accent, "Get to work." she motions to the empty desk. I awkwardly walk over and sit down, looking at the familiar characters on the machine.

I put some paper in the machine and look at the first paper in the stack, all in another language, but familiar in characters. I set the paper on the tray next to the machine and, slowly, type it out, letter by letter.

One of the girls leans over to me, "the girls are going out after this, you're welcome to come with us," she lets me know, "And you'll get to be pretty fast at this in time."

"Oh, thank you," I reply, as she leans back into her work.

"Ugh," one of the girls sighs, "Time's up for the day."

I choke a little, looking at my significantly smaller pile of copied papers compared to hers. "Leave the paper there, the next girl will get it," she says, "Come on, come out with us."

"Okay," I look at the half-done paper sitting there in the machine, "Where are you guys going?"

"Oh, to the bar," she says, "You see some *pretty* soldiers sometimes." I blush a little and pick up the stack of papers to straighten them.

"Oh," she goes on the say something in Jermain, "You already have one in mind."

"I really don't," I persist, "I'm just in a transition period in this country."

"Then prove it and come with us, there'll be dancing," she says.

"I never said no," I say, "But I'm not looking for a man." I straighten the papers and stand up, faltering on the heels. She motions and almost all girls look ready to go. They all start murmuring about themselves in different languages amongst themselves.

They all, in perfect unison, say, "Hail Hister!" and raise their arms up. The boss lady does it in reply and they all look at me.

"Oh, right," I whisper, "Uh, Hail *Hister.*"

"*Heil Hister!*" the lady replies and we all start funneling out.

I walk up next to the girl who speaks Anglish and match her walking speed, nearly breaking my ankle in the process. "So, uh, are you the only one who speaks Anglish?" I ask.

"Two other girls do," she confesses, "But not as well as me. Where are you from, *Charlie?*"

I remember the name badges and look at hers, not able to read it, "Greenwich, but I'd rather not talk about it-"

The girls all look back at me like I'm a ghost or something, but the girl shoos them away. "I wouldn't either," she says, "My name's Edith."

"Thanks, *Edith*," I say as we come by the workers in the front foyer.

"Hail Hister," they all stop and repeat, with the workers standing and replying.

"Oh, uh, Hail Hister," I raise my arm, but I catch a glimpse of the man who walked me in, officer's hat and monocle.

"With conviction!" He raises her hand and stomps his foot, "Hail Hister!"

I clear my throat and raise my hand in embarrassment. "Hail!" I cough, "*Hister.*"

He smiles and lowers his arm, "Good enough for today." The girls start moving out and the workers back to their job.

Edith grabs my arm and pulls me along, nearly tripping me. "The bar is around the corner," she says, "there'll be dancing if there's a nice song and a *nice* man."

"Oh, fun," I awkwardly go about accepting this, "Where are all the male-workers?"

We make our way down these enraging steps. "Fighting the war," she replies, "But they get frequent motherland leave." we turn the corner and she points out the building with flashing lights in the window and a sign with a strange little man dancing.

She pulls me along across the street and into the building. I breathe in the oddly palatable smell of beer and whatnot compared to my old job at Betty's. The girls start funneling in behind us and everyone drunkenly hails us inside.

"I think I should-" I begin to make an excuse to go back to Charles' mother's, but she yanks me further into the establishment. She and the bartender exchange in Jermain and he walks off.

"What do you drink?" She asks.

"I don't, uh, I'm not a drinker," I tell her.

"*Saft!*" she yells.

"What's that," I ask, looking around to see a band playing music in the corner.

"Here," she hands me a juice box, "No good-lookers today,"

I look at the box in confusion, breaking down and opening it. The clock on the wall reads almost 5 o'clock. "I really should be going, Edith," I tell her, sipping some of the fruit juice.

"Aw," she pouts, "Walk safely, Charlie."

I wave my hand and make my way back *home*. The doors close behind me and a cold gust of wind hits me. I look up to see the silver man dawning on the city for a moment as my eyes adjust to a clock tower in the distance.

I brush it off and keep frantically walking through the street, like the face of the clock is about to shoot a ray of death when a car horn breaks my delusion. I brush it off and keep on going before the sun sets below the concrete jungles.

I take the key, and for the first time, open the door to my new apartment. The door swings open and I smell that fresh carpet smell. I take a step in and take in the empty room. Jessica looks over my shoulder and her mother smack my bottom, pushing through all of us. I shriek in surprise and move over for the lady.

"It's nice," Jessica says, "But it's super small."

"Well," I try to justify it, "I'm just one person."

Her mother starts going off in her language and exchanges with Jessica. "She says it's no place to raise kids," she translates.

I pucker my lips and I may be blushing, "Well, It's below budget and I'll be able to save money." I pull out my little wallet-purse and pull out my checkbook, soon to be stopped by their mother's hand.

"No," she whispers, sliding it back into my purse.

"Oh, uh, *Danke*," I say.

"Try again," Jessica says.

"Is that not the right word?" I look at her confused as the little girl is dancing around on the carpet.

"We should get going," she says, "I have studying to do."

"Yeah," I look at my watch, "I have to head to work too.

"Thank you guys so much for everything."

Their mother pats my cheek and they all make their way out and back home. I recount the twists and turns that is my new on-foot commute as I walk down the concrete steps.

I make my way to work, correctly remembering the turns and the streets. I've been studying the dictionary, but I don't recognize a single street name. But I do make it there, walking up the steps at an angle so I can make two steps each.

I walk through the door, and *Herr Stampfen* stomps his foot and shouts, "Hail Hister."

I raise my arm in never ending shame, "Hail, Hister." He accepts it and I walk down the hall to my desk. I've gotten considerably faster at copying the documents in a language I'm only a beginner at, but nowhere near the speed of the other girls.

I sit down at my desk and look at the time; right on the clock. I start working, taking the first page on the stack. I look at the title, labeled *Torwächter*, a pair of words familiar to me. I make out a few words of the document, but nothing I can understand. Edith walks in and sits next to me and starts going at it on the typewriter.

The day goes on and I see *Torwächter* an unreasonable amount of times. "Careful, those are sensitive documents," *Herr Stampfen* whispers behind me, making me jump in my chair.

"Oh, yes," I say, going back to work.

"I've received a telephone message for you," he says, "In regards to the health of one *Charles.*" I stop my typing and see that he's holding out his hand, meaning for me to come with him.

I stand up and follow him into the hallway. "He's currently staying in the military hospital; he specifically requested that you be informed that he's, quote, 'been shot in the back and the ass.'"

"Oh," I sit there, speechless.

"If you'd like to go to him, I can arrange a vehicle pickup for you right now."

"That-that'd be great, actually," I start to panic a little on the inside assuming the worst that he might die.

He puts his hand on my back, pushing me along to the front of the building where there's a military vehicle just waiting there at the bottom of the steps. He leads me down the awkward steps and opens the door for me to get in. He says something to two men sitting in there already.

"Hail Hister!" they say to each other, before we start to drive off.

"So, you headed to hospital too, shnookums-" the other soldier slaps the back of his head whilst I sit there in some sort of shock.

"Just drive, dumbnut!" the other man says. Before I know it, we arrive, but I just stare at the building.

Why am I feeling like this? I ask myself, *I barely know the guy.*

"Hey shnookums-" the driver gets slapped again, "You want me to walk you in?" the other soldier punches his face and he falls down to the ground.

"You want to check in yourself?" he shouts, "I'm sorry for him, he forgot how to be a gentleman."

"Yeah, it's fine," I say, walking myself to the door. My arms get cold and a shadow dawns on me. I feel the cold gaze of the silver man as I look behind me to find the other soldier opening the door for me. "Oh, uh, *danke,*" I say, walking in.

"Um," He rushes in behind me, "Who are you here to see? You seem a little out of it."

"Charles," I tell him. He walks up to the desk and I just keep on walking further into the complex.

"She's here for, uh, *Charles*," he says to the desk lady. She gives him directions to the room, but I just keep walking on. The soldier rushes beside me and places his hand on my back to guide me.

He opens a door revealing a room with bed after bed all next to each other separated by curtains. I look around and see his family standing and talking around him.

"Oh!" Jessica sees me, walking over to me, "Charles! Charlie is here!"

I look over around the curtain to see him with a tube in his arm. "Hey!" he says, speech slurred, "Charlie!"

"Hey," I walk over, "Charles; you're alive."

He starts laughing and a sense of relief washes over me as I see him in good enough condition. "It was only 3 bullets, they fished 'em out. They're letting me keep one," he says, shaking a cup with a mushroomed bullet inside.

"That's, uh," I pause, "nice." I rub my face and try to wake up from this weird dream.

A nurse walks up to me, "He'll be alright, no worries."

"Guys," he starts, "You have no idea how high I am on morphine right now." he shakes his head a little and sets the bullet cup down.

"He's been talking crap for hours," Jessica tells me, being slapped in the back of the head by her mother, followed by some exchange between them.

I put my hands on my head, "I'm just glad you're alright Charles."

"He's glad you're here," Jessica tells me, "He's just out of it. Visiting hours are almost done, we'll have you over for dinner when he's ready to come home."

"I appreciate you visiting me, Charlie," he says as I help him down into the hospital bed, "How have you been adjusting?"

"I'm adjusting," I tell him, "The girls at work are nice; my new place is, to be honest, better than my place at Greenwich.

"I actually have a phone now."

"You mean you didn't have a phone in Greenwich?" he asks.

"I was pinching pennies, okay!?" I say, stretching my arms, "Betty's didn't pay well; jobs were stretched thin by the war."

"I'm sorry about that, by the way. It's rough being displaced."

"Honestly," I confess, "My life is better here."

"Charlie," he goes on whispering, scratching his head, "Do you know why I fight for something I don't believe in?

"It's because, for the sake of my family, it's better to be safe than to be right sometimes."

Deep down, I know it. I playfully punch his arm. "It's just conflicting sometimes-"

"Not for me," he says, "I'd rather be on the winning side of this war."

"How do you know Hister is going to win?" I ask, "I witnessed one of the Amerian bombs first hand-"

He pulls me close, "Because with the power of the Gate Guardian, he can do it! You saw that first hand too."

"Where did he even find the *Gate Guardian*?" I ask, sitting down next to him, "Like when does something like that even exist?"

"There's this *foundation* that was keeping it under wraps in the Middle East; Hister is just making it chase an olive branch."

The cold winter wind blows down my neck, reminding me to buy a winter coat. I knock on the family door, and Charles opens up the door in fully dawned in his army uniform.

"Come on in," he welcomes me. I walk in and catch a glimpse of their intellavision; a map with a red line going up from Arabia all the way into Angland and back down a little.

"Hey Charlie!' Jessica greets me, with the little girl waving to me, "My mother made some pasta."

"Oh great!" I walk in, rubbing my arms to get warm, "Can't remember the last time I had pasta."

"Oh! And Charles got a melted chunk of concrete from Londen," she sounds excited, "It's totally rad."

"Jess," he motions to her to stop. He walks me in and pulls out a chair for me.

"So what's with the uniform?" I ask, sitting down.

"Jessica likes it when I wear it," he replies, sitting down next to me.

"I like the hat," she juts in, "I think it's cool."

"Mama!" Charles starts exchanging with his mother. For the life of me, regardless of how much I study the dictionary, cannot understand that woman. Their mother brings a big pan full of pasta, and Jessica starts serving herself only to be stopped from a slap on the hand.

Charles starts making a plate and sets it in front of me. "Oh thank you," I say as he makes another plate.

"How's work treating you?" he asks, handing the plate across to Jessica.

"Oh, it's just like if you were copying papers in a language you don't know," I say, "Something along those lines."

"Is that what they're having you do? Pay well?"

"Yeah, you could say that," I reply. He grabs my hand, and for a brief moment of confusion I stall before he starts praying over the food. I quickly bow my head and watch around me to see Jessica making a face at me. We eat, enjoy the meal. Charles tells me it's homemade.

I open the door, being greeted with an icy gust of wind blowing into my uncovered face, but my arms are protected by my new winter coat I splurged on. It's a nice shade of dark red with a brown fur lining.

I look about, not seeing traffic making its way through the street, though I do see an automobile speeding down, and it's gone in blink of an eye. The phone starts ringing, but I close the door and make my commute to work.

The streets are almost empty, nearly no persons, just the occasional vehicle going down the street. I think to myself, *Why is no one here?*

I come to the steps of my workplace and I see an empty foyer. I rush up the steps, making one leap of a step after another up to the tinted glass door.

I cup my hand around my eyes to try to peer into the building, looking for a clock thinking I'm earlier than usual; before opening. But no, the clock ticks on time. *Oh, no,* I tell myself, *Not again...*

The revving of an engine grows too loud from the background and *CRASH!* The army truck flies up the steps as I turn to see the commotion.

One of the men starts shouting at me in Jermain. "I don't-" I try to say.

"God is striking!" he says, jumping out and chasing after me. He just sweeps me up and runs over back to the vehicle and sets me in.

"Charlie?!" Charles looks at me, "What the hell are you doing? You didn't pick up the phone!"

The vehicle jumps and then starts driving away. He grabs my face to stare at him, but I look behind him to see the silver man.

"Don't look at him," he shouts as I try to move his hands, "Look at me, Charlie!"

"What-Why," I start to trip over my words, "He-he's here; why is he-"

BOOM! I see the ray of death burning the clock tower down, and the silver man pushing the building next to it. I scream, but Charles covers my ears, but it's too late, I've been tipped over the edge.

My heart starts beating hard through my ears and my arms grow cold. The ray of death sweeps behind us, melting and burning the buildings and road. The driver curses and swerves to turn onto an interstate to the next city.

I start to panic and rock back and forth. *BOOM!* An explosion goes off behind us, spraying some gravel into the truck. Charles Grabs my face again, "Look at me!" he shouts over the ray of death, "You're still my top priority! Stay calm-"

The ray beams out in front of us, melting the road and blinding me as I look to it. The driver swerves to the right, knocking the other soldiers over.

I look up to see the city on fire, and Amerian planes off in the distance. "They-The Amerians," I point my finger.

"Look at me!" Charles points my face at him, "They're the last hope of controlling this thing- *Everything* will be okay!" I look at him, deep in his eyes as he wants me to believe him.

But I don't. *BOOM!* The ray crashes right next to us, pushing the car to the side. We get knocked out and land on the dirt side of the road. The soldiers hop back onto their feet and rush to go push the truck back right side up, leaving me to stare into the eyes of death.

"Heave!" they all shout, pushing the truck over.

The Amerians are right over head, distracting the silver man: The Gate Guardian. The planes begin to raid their bombs upon the The Gate Guardian; it's brighter than the sun as the explosions go off in red fireballs.

The guardian slaps one of the plans out of the air as I look upon the big-plane, the one that drops the city-erasing bombs. I'm unable to close my eyes as I watch the plane approach, but I pray nonetheless, saying my last goodbyes to this world. The truck's engine sounds like it stuck and Charles runs up to me, wrapping his arms around me, telling me to close my eyes.

Notes on 0-0-1 The Gate Guardian

⊶⊙⊷

"0-0-1 The Gate Guardian: Destruction of The Axis" is based on "SCP-001 Proposal CODENAME: Dr. Clef – The Gate Guardian" By "DrClef": http://scp-wiki.wikidot.com/dr-clef-s-proposal

"0-0-1 The Gate Guardian: Destruction of The Axis" and only this single work is licensed under CC-BY-SA 3.0. All other works in this publication are Copyright © 2020 by BC. Neon

⊶⊙⊷

Hero Sub: The End

My comrades are unconscious, laying on the ground beside me. I'm too weak to fight any more against this great evil. The 4 of us together had enough might and power to end this, I thought. But he's too strong.

The world-ender sits there, rebuilding his body from the surrounding earth as just from his single skull. *CRASH!* Boulders are falling from the sky as I'm too weak to alter the gravity of this region anymore. *CRASH!* I use the last of my energy to save my comrades from the falling debris.

The world-ender begins to laugh as his organs are being constructed from dirt. "You still weren't enough!" he says.

I say a prayer that my old master will come back to save us, but no one's been able to contact or locate him in years, I doubt he's even on Earth. *CRASH!* Another boulder hits the ground.

"You did good, kid," I hear a familiar voice. The debris stops falling for a moment. The world-ender turns around and sees his defeat. He starts haphazardly constructing his body as quickly as he can.

But that's all I see, and with a gargantuan display of ultimate power, everyone is whisked away from the battlefield. All the heroes at the base of the mountain, all the villains they're fighting. I find myself, a safe distance away, but still in view.

A bright flash of light at the summit where we fought, bright and warm as the sun itself. But I doubt that's killed the world-ender, he's survived something like it before.

I use my ability to see what's going on, and I hear the muffled dialogue between the two. Then, nothing. Space begins to warp and the entire battlefield shimmers until it's zipped up in a massive portal to someplace else. The landscape is forever changed as the mountain disappears, leaving a crater deep enough to capture the world-ender's last essence beneath the Earth's crust.

The hole left behind must be the size of a small country, and I'm just at the cusp of falling in.

I make a bridge between this world and Earth, stepping through to see my old apprentice holding on for the dear life of those who fought beside her. A stone falls from the sky and she deflects it away from their unconscious bodies.

I stop all the debris from their fight where it is and say, "You did good kid," before sending them off to a safe distance.

My old rival, my friend begins assimilating material into his body as fast as he can to face me in our final match.

"You have the universe in your eyes, don't you," he manages to say, "Is there anything you can't see?"

"No."

I open a bridge to the Solar Core underneath him, blasting him away to oblivion, and I know it's not enough, but I wanted to hear his screams of torment.

I take a moment to sense where his body extends to, and I take all the landmass he occupies and send the both of us to a remote planet I discovered in my travels. Something void of importance and life.

All this earth begins to fall to the surface from the low orbit of this planet. I form a safe platform for me to descend with. His body comes crawling out of this mountain, holding on to it to prepare for impact.

"I searched the cosmos for lifetimes, beyond what the human mind can comprehend in search of *your* defeat," I announce.

"Is that so?" He assimilates material and sends his needles up to me for an attack. He screams, "Did you find it!?"

The air behind to heat up from reentry, and I shatter his needles with a simple wave of a hand. The mass of stone and dirt begins breaking up, shattering beneath his feet whilst I remain safe.

"Yes," I command. He attempts to hold the mass with his spindles, absorbing even more material to build his body.

"You're full of cheap tricks!" he sens more needles at me, but I expand the space between me and them. "I am the mighty *World-Eater!* I shall consume this 'cosmos' of yours for myself!"

I transport large stones from the falling mass and drop them on him, one after another. "Show me, World-Eater, and I shall show you the Sun!"

He assimilates the columns by his overwhelming power, but I keep sending more at him to distract him. His spindles reach out from the sides, but I release the power of this world's sun's nuclear core in two spots on either side, melting the mass along with the power of reentry.

Even still I hear his screams of pain. I close the bridges as the mass breaks in three smaller pieces, no longer being held together by his power.

I step through a bridge and grab ahold of his reforming throat, creating a barrier between us and the impact of the masses hitting the surface. He attempts to feed off of me, but I know better and prepared.

The land and sky scapes have changed dramatically; we're showered with intense radiation. I allow him to assimilate my hand. "Allow me to end this," I say, creating the largest bridge I've ever attempted as the stars in the sky begin disappearing from our sight. The bridge transports us into the home of a nebula close to the galactic core.

"You were just toying with me," I feel the vibrations in his throat. I finally see the defeat in his eyes, "I never stood a chance."

"I was trying to feel something again," I admit to it. His power reaches up to my arm as he desperately tries to survive, "The only reason you lost is you attempted to throw away your humanity to become a being of higher power.

"And you succeeded.

"You never stood for anything, you never had an end goal."

"And you did?" he retorts as I begin creating a gravity well, pulling in surrounding interstellar material upon us, "You'll only kill me if you die too."

"A *hero* must make sacrifices," I quote my old apprentice, who in hindsight was greater than I ever could've been. I release the universe from my eyes and look upon the failure of my closest friend with my own vision, the only one who could've understood what it was like to stand miles above anyone else.

The universe flashes before us as this solar system I've moved consumed by the event horizon of a new quasar forms with us at the very center.

⊷ ⊙ ⊶

I look up at the sky with my *friends* and witness the birth of a new star in the tapestry of the universe, knowing the world-ender and my old master were no more.

Into The Mystic

Sequel to Into The Wildlands

I take my fire-roasted meat from the burning fire and set it aside. I look to Omuru, whose conversing with one of the natives out here, letting his meat cook longer in the fire. I never understand his appetite; he likes his meat burned basically to a crisp and eats any berry that he finds laying around regardless of how poisonous it may be.

"Omuru," I call out to him, "Don't burn your food, that's a prime cut." But he disregards me. I take a bite out of my food and try to savor it. This animal came from the Mystic and the taste is noticeably *different*, but not in a bad way.

I sign to one of the natives, asking about the boat. *Is it repaired yet?* I ask him.

He signs back, saying, *No, no good trees to cut from.*

I take another bite of the meat, enjoying the hardy smell of the fire. "Omuru, how far are away from the wall, again?"

Omuru pauses for a moment, thinking, "50 miles, Scott."

"I thought we were traveling more these past few days?"

"We must go around the Mystic, not through it," he replies.

"I understand that," I persist, "But we haven't moved anymore since last week-"

"The Mystic is big, Scott, bigger than the city."

The native signs at me, *Mystic not safe, go around. Too big.*

I sign back, *I know, how big?*

He shrugs his shoulders, not knowing the answer to my question. I take another bite and afix my stick into the ground. "Well, what are we going to do tomorrow?"

"We'll travel that way," Omuru points towards the city.

"What do you mean? That's exactly where we don't want to go-"

"You're growing complacent, Scott; don't forget who's superior here," he continues to remind me, "Rest tonight, travel tomorrow."

I pick my food back up and finish it off before I walk away to find a soft place to sleep. The night goes on and the fire dies out, the talking subsides.

I'm carried off into a dream; I dream of the possible life with Jennifer I could've had if I had just done things right, just done things a little different. I haven't seen her delicate face in years, I miss her as the days go on.

Something feels like it is choking me, constricting my entire body. Suddenly, I'm picked up. I open my eyes to see Omuru holding me underneath his arm. I try to speak, but nothing escapes my lips. He holds me tight as he runs through this fog.

The natives are also running with us, chanting in their strange language, running between the trees. Omuru, on the other hand, barrels through the trees, knocking them down with his enormous stature.

The mist begins to clear as we travel further until we hit a clearing and Omuru tosses me to the ground. I'm finally able to take a breath and begin coughing,

"Wha-" I try to say, catching my breath.

"The Mystic's fog was expanding," he explains, "I forgot that you are not adapted for it."

"What- what the hell?" I manage to subside my coughing long enough to say something, "Since when is there killer fog waiting out here-"

"That's what the outer wall was built for," he replies, "But you'd never know that." My coughing comes back, and as I look at my hand, there's blood from my mouth.

"Why are they alright?" I ask him, getting back up to my feet.

Adapted, the native signs to me.

"They've adapted over hundreds of years," Omuru explains to me.

The sun barely shines through the thick forest above. Clearings are rare, and it seems the Mystic is bordering everywhere we go. Omuru assures everybody there's a path around it, but I've grown skeptical, but not daring to confront a being who could punch me in half.

I stare fervently at a still animal, ready to hunt and secure food for the evening. *Ready... Ready,* I think, only to be blindsided by my native friend propelling a spear through the head of the doe, chanting something.

I had it! I sign to him, but he shrugs his shoulder walking over to our dinner. We walk together back to camp, where Omuru stands out, nearly glowing in the faint light of the jungle.

"Omuru!" I call out, "How far are we today?"

"40 miles," he calls back.

"40?!" I rush over, "Why are we getting closer?!"

"The Mystic is herding us in-" he pauses.

"You talk about it like it's a living person!" he turns and grabs me by the throat, lifting me up to eye level to exert his dominance.

"Don't forget who stands above the other." He lowers me back to my feet and lets me go, allowing me to breathe again. "The Mystic acts on its own."

Mark, as I've come to call him, signs to me, preaching some lore from his tribe. He tells me it's like a great snake.

The day goes on, the sun sets and the dark of the night creeps up on us. I start a fire to cook the meat that was caught today. The natives begin a dance around the fire as I stand back and wait for the food to cook in the pleasantly smelling fire.

One of them breaks formation and pulls out a spear, doing one of their chants and throws it into the night. I hear a woman scream and a BANG! All the natives start scattering around and Mark bravely runs towards the woman in the night. There's some commotion and the sound of resistance as they come into the light.

My eyes must be tired, or the fire's playing a trick on me. "Jennifer?" I ask, signing to Mark to let her go.

City dweller, he signs, *Dangerous*. He tosses a gun to Omuru's feet.

I walk over there to get a better look, and it is. "Jennifer? Wha- what are you doing out here?" I try to embrace her, but Omuru holds out his hand, stopping me.

"State your business, girl," he commands, in his own language.

She responds fluently, "I'm just here to find someone out here."

I sit her down by the fire to warm her icy hands. "You're telling me society collapsed?" I ask to ensure my sanity.

"When word got out, that one of us escaped," he breathes into her hands to warm them, "And even more so, an Osheky up and leaving, everything went to *crap-*

"learned that word from Grenand."

"How did-how did you recover?" I ask, "I saw you shot. Twice!"

He pulls down the shoulder on her clothes, showing me the scar from the bullet. "They pulled me back through and I got to see the forbidden hospital before everything collapsed; when I got out, they were hanging Grenand through the streets."

I look over to Omuru, glaring down Jennifer. "What about all the Osheky in the inner ring?"

"They've been trying to maintain order, but they're in shambles too."

Omuru stands up and walks over, grabbing me by my clothes and dragging me off into darkness not lit by the fire. "She's lying-"

"Then why would she be out here?" he looks very carefully at me, twitching his eyes.

"Jennifer, 91-42!" He shouts out. He marches over back into the light. She looks back up at him in a sweat.

"That would be my number," she says in Osheky language.

All the natives are looking back and forth between the two as they talk, though I'm not sure if they understand. "Why are you really here?"

"I thought you two might still be out here," he replies, "Once I found the first dead animal, you guys were easy to find." Omuru twitches his eyes in disbelief. He leans down from his towering height until he at eye level and whispers something into her ear, instantly changing the look in her eyes.

"I call that guy Mark," I point to him, signing to him.

Girlfriend? He signs back to me, but I shake my head.

She looks intently at his hands, maybe she knows what it means. She's constantly looking around at the individuals in our caravan.

"How did Grenand die?" Omuru asks her.

"A group of workers tied something around her neck and pulled her up and paraded around," she explains, "Along with other officials."

"Do you know of the Mystic?" he asks.

"It would," she pauses looking behind her, "Come up in research papers I read, but not really."

Omuru stops her and pulls me along by my shirt. "Hey! What are-"

"Whisper," he commands me, "She's not Jennifer-"

"What do you mean?!" I retort, lowering my voice. I look back at her walking behind us, admiring the jungle.

"She's lying-" Omuru tells me, right before throwing me further into the mist. I crash into some mud and the natives look on me in humor, some of them laughing. Mark signs to me, laughing.

But when I take a deep breath in, it feels like I swallowed the spikes we use for hunting. Mark rushes over and holds my mouth shut to keep from breathing in more of the mist. I look over to Jennifer holding her hand out to touch the mist but retracts quickly.

Black figures emerge from the shadows; men dressed in black with their faces covered, brandishing guns. I see some floating contraptions making their appearance. Through the trees, they come.

"Halt right there," they say, "You'll die if you go in there."

Shivers start making their way up and down my spine, and I see my arm discoloring. "Come on Jennifer," Omuru shouts, "They're lying; they can't follow you in here!"

One of the men holds something up in their hand; something with a red button, keeping their thumb raised above it. She looks back and just freezes there. She takes a step back and the man presses down.

"No!" She cries out, "Not again, I'm sorry!" she arches her back and falls to the ground. She starts scratching her arms, but it turns to flailing her arms about, trying to back away from the approaching men.

She screams in pain and writhes around in the dirt, making her way from the man. Omuru rushes over and pulls her beyond the threshold of the Mystic's fog.

Once she's consumed by it she calms down, being carried by Omuru down towards the group. I take another painful breath, like something cutting through my insides, spitting blood from my mouth.

"Move in," one of the men say, marching forward; the flying mechanisms cross the Mystic's threshold and just fall down to the ground, crackling.

One of the natives throws a spear, skewers one of the three men through his torso and pinning him to the ground. "Leave him, he'll dissolve before we make it back," the leader tells the other one.

Everyone starts to walk deeper and deeper in the mist-infected jungle. The fog becomes too thick to see, but Mark grabs me by the arm.

"Omuru!" the mist clears enough for me to see Jennifer getting dropped to the ground kicking and screaming, and promptly covering her mouth to keep from breathing.

I fall to my knees, trying to get all the blood out of my system, but it just keeps hurting. Jennifer rushes to my side. "*You* don't need to hold your breath, 91-42," Omuru says.

"He's going to die," she finally starts breathing. My vision starts blurring as I stare down at the pool of blood forming on the ground.

Spears start flying around us, seemingly from all directions. *BANG!* Omuru picks up both of us and starts running into the fog. The trees seem to dissolve away in the mist, leaving a clearing all around.

One of the men screams in defeat, assuming death.

The mist has completely paralyzed me, but I catch a glimpse of Jennifer being unaffected by it, and unsurprisingly Omuru too. *BANG!* The gun goes off, and spears fly around above us and the final man screams his last breath.

I see the body of the man pinned to the ground with the spear wandering by us. More blood starts flowing from my mouth, dripping on the ground, sprouting seedlings where it pools upon the ground.

"Don't try to make sense of anything in here, you'll go insane," Omuru tells us.

"He's going to die," Jennifer cries out for me, reaching for my limp body. I catch a glimpse of my arm, basically glowing yellow with my blood vessels moving around like snakes underneath the soil. "Why am I alright out here?"

Tears flow down her face and I try to reach out, but I'm unable to move an inch. "We're almost through," he reminds us.

The Mist becomes thinner and thinner until I can vaguely see the sun above, but it begins to twain. The mist finally leaves and I see a landscape of grass without a tree in sight. Feeling comes back in my limbs and I take a deep breath in, coughing all the blood out on the grass. Omuru flat out drops us in the grass and Jennifer rushes to my side.

"You're sad copy of the original," he calls out, "Created by private Osheky research-"

She looks up at him, in tears, "How could you say that?!" I reach up to grab her, but I slip and pull down the back of the shoulder on her shirt, revealing smooth skin, no bullet wound.

Omuru explained that Osheky in the inner wall were able to create people from nothing; something I couldn't understand, but Jennifer looked uncomfortably familiar with it. He said Jennifer was shot through the neck, killing her instantly.

Jennifer also spilled her secrets; she was commissioned by Sir Lakewell, the leader of our civilization, personally to bring me back along with Omuru, but failed and is no longer able to go back. Although, there was much unrest in the public since we made a hole in the outer wall and just walked out.

"I just remember taking the first step out and something went through my shoulder and I woke up in a white room," she continues.

"That white room was part of a cloning chamber in the inner ring," he says, "The chamber can't replicate scars; they must be *artificially* induced."

It still feels my lungs were cut out of my chest, but I can at least breathe and move my fingers once again. "Omuru," I begin to cough, "Where are we?"

He looks at me and smiles, "We're on the other side."

"Omuru," I clear my throat, "That explains *shit*.

"Where are we?" I command.

"The Mystic is a connection between two worlds," he explains, motioning off into the distance to a white tower, "Mine to yours." The hum of a vehicle grows ever louder, and off in the horizon I see something getting closer.

"What-what about all the natives?" I persist, "Where'd they go?"

The vehicle comes to a screeching stop a little ways away, some creature only a dream could create exits. He approaches and Omuru twitches his eyes.

As he comes into our vicinity, he starts shouting in Osheky language. Omuru stands and approaches him.

"You're not welcome here, Osheky-" Omuru grabs him by his hair and smashes his face into his knee, multiple times before tossing him to the side. Blood drains from his mouth as he looks back up.

"Don't forget who is superior," Omuru spits down on him. He over to the vehicle and kicks it to the side, digging into the grassy soil.

"Damn you Osheky!" the creature shouts, before charging Omuru, pulling out a sharp blade. But Omuru quickly disarms him and holds him up by his throat, crushing down until the body goes limp.

"Pestering filth," Omuru grits his teeth, tossing to the limp body to the side.

"Omuru!" Jennifer calls out, "You can't just-" she screams in unrest. "I'm just- I'm tired of people dying already!"

I finally get up on my feet, spitting more blood down to the ground. "Omuru, where are we going?"

"To what you call a hospital," he barks at me, "Now walk with us."

Jennifer helps me to my feet underneath my arm and we make our way further into the grassland. Clouds begin to form overhead, obscuring the twin suns. Omuru is staying ahead of us, sloshing in the mud that keeps getting deeper every step.

"So, we're on another world?" I ask Jennifer.

"Yes," she responds, "I suppose."

"And Omuru is not native to Earth?"

"It would seem that way," she giggles a little, "You really never paid attention to history."

"No, can't say that I did-" I trip a little in the mud, splashing it up on my legs.

The town is white; everything plastered white. The people here are even dressed in lightly covered reds, blues, and tans, a long call from what Omuru wore back in the city. Omuru draws eyes from everyone passing by, herding what I would assume to be children away from him. He's dressed in worn-out brown, covered in holes and mud.

Someone official-looking stops Omuru and they start speaking together. "Your kind isn't welcome here anymore-" he tries to say before Omuru readies a fist and launches him into the ground. The ground cracks on impact and the creature just twitching about on the ground.

I cough a little, blood spewing on my arm. We continue on our way, turning a few corners until he enters a building. When we follow inside, people are in terrifying awe at him, and then their eyes turn to us in curiosity.

"Who are they?" someone asks.

"They're from the other side!" another person answers.

Omuru starts demanding that they give me something. They refuse and Omuru picks them up to eye level.

"Omuru," Jennifer boldly calls out, "Violence isn't always the answer." Omuru sets the person at the desk down and brushes out the wrinkles in his shirt. "My friend needs medicine," Jennifer says out loud, drawing attention to us. They all start murmuring amongst themselves, asking how they know their language.

Omuru continues talking to the one at the desk, saying some technical things I can't understand. "Alright!" he says, "But you're kind won't come back."

The one at the desk waves his hand at me, and Jennifer pulls me along through a doorway and into a room. "Is this what Osheky have been up to?" he asks, pointing to Jennifer.

"What do you mean?" I reply.

He sets some medical instrument on my chest and a small screen reads out some written information. I've been away far too long to be adequate in written scripts. "She's been engineered, unlike you," he informs us.

"What do you mean?" Jennifer asks him.

"Mhm," he groans, going out of the room.

Another walks with a vile with a long thin piece of metal in hand. "Wha-" I try to say, before she jabs the shard into my neck. A strange sound reverberates up my neck into my ears.

"Ah," I push the creature away, pulling the metal from my throat, "What the hell?"

The creature braces herself on the wall and says, "Give it a week, you'll feel better. Now leave before you cause more trouble." She steps up and walks out the door.

I start coughing into my arm, further staining it with blood from my innards. Jennifer looks at me and lets out a single laugh, "What in the world are we doing?"

"We're free," I tell her, "Free to do what our hearts desire."

"If I- if *she* didn't hesitate, *she* would've been there with you," she says, rubbing her shoulder, "I didn't even know the scar wasn't on my back."

"Honestly-"

Omuru walks in, interrupting our conversation. "We better leave before they force us out." he grabs me and yanks me along his extended steps through this hospital. He still draws eyes as we leave to the outside.

I pull off his hand and falter in my steps, "I can walk by myself. I'm not totally disabled."

"Where to now?" Jennifer asks.

"Back through the Mystic," he replies, "As long as Scott has that medicine running through him, he'll survive."

"Now, Omuru!" I shout, Jennifer rushing to be between Omuru and I. Omuru looks back at me in a very threatening manner, "Why would we go back? I- I kind of like it here."

"You'll never be happy here, always looking over your shoulder."

"Is that why Osheky-" Jennifer turns around and puts her hand over my mouth.

"Don't overdo it, Scott."

⊷⊙⊷

We approach the vehicle that Omuru dismantled earlier, Omuru tearing off the back door to the cabin. We try to catch up to him to see what he's doing, but he just steps back out with a black box in hand.

"What's-"

"It's a measuring device to help guide us through the Mystic."

I try to look past his gargantuan body inside the vehicle, but Omuru seems to keep obscuring the view. A cold wind starts blowing from the Mystic and Omuru gets a big smile on his white face.

We march on through the grass, moving past the dead body into the deadly fog. I stop right before entering the fog, "Are you sure?"

Omuru turns and grabs me by the back of the neck and pulls me beyond the threshold. I breathe in the mist and my lungs start burning, just not as bad. Jennifer rests her hand on my back as I control my coughing.

The black box starts beeping in different tones and spacing, with Omuru making erratic movements in the mist, reminiscent of when Jennifer would try to avoid camera views in school, but we keep him in our sights. There's still a small and steady burning in my chest and my skin is turning yellow.

"It-" I cough, "didn't take this long to get through last time!" the wind starts blowing hard and the mist consumes our vision and we lose sight of Omuru.

A hand grabs my shoulder and I look back to see Omuru marching on behind us, "Stay close, a storm is coming through."

Jennifer grabs hold his garment and interlocks her hand in mind as we brave this storm. An elk comes into view as the wind blows open a clearing. It looks at us and it twains as two elk run off in different directions leaving behind a rapidly growing tree sapling.

Omuru pulls us along a strange path, and slowly the mist clears up, revealing the jungle. We start trudging through mud from the river and the mist recedes behind us and I begin to breathe clearly again.

Omuru starts making one of the native's special calls into the dimly lit jungle. Surprisingly someone calls back and people begin to emerge from the trees and I see an older Mark coming through, signing to me.

You've been gone so long, he signs to me, *You haven't aged*.

He comes close and we embrace. *How long was it?* I ask him.

7 years, he tells me. He motions that we follow, but Omuru is still meandering on a strange path, going past everyone.

"Hey, Omuru!" I call out to him.

"I'm finding something, Scott, don't interrupt me." I place Mark to the side and chase after him. He stops shy of something, and tears a tree in half, revealing the long-familiar concrete of the outer wall. "I have to know what's inside."

"We *know* what's on the other side, Omuru," I try to tell him, "The same dictator crap, just 7 years older and angrier; do you think Grenand is going to just let you in?"

"Omuru, we can't just wander back in there," Jennifer continues on, "They'll arrest even you-"

"Listen," he tells me, putting the side of his head to the wall. I follow and listen and hear rumbling coming from the other side. Nothing I know could be making that sound.

"Let's find the entrance," Omuru says to me.

"There isn't-"

"There is, going straight from the inner wall to the Wildlands."

"Omuru, You're insane," Jennifer says, "We'll all be arrested or worse!"

Omuru grins, "We could set all of them free, just like us."

7 Levels Deep

"Okay,"

"Yes?"

"So, I'll give you a rundown of what's going to happen: there are 7 layers of subconsciousness," I begin, "I'll be using a specific list of spells specially designed to bring you, or your consciousness, down to each level."

"Okay."

"Let's begin." My patient outreaches his hands, and I slowly mark down the spells on them. The spells are perfectly drawn; I've done this a hundred times. I place my hands over his, and cast the spells, just like I've done before. We find ourselves in an infinite shoreline; a grand ocean to the right and mountains to the left.

"Where are we?" he asks.

"This is the first level," I explain, "It is an abstract representation of your mood. You said you're bipolar, correct?"

"Yes, ma'am," he replies.

"Then we should go a level deeper before a storm comes, so I can do my best work."

"A what?"

I take hold of his hands, but fail to cast the spells, as the spells are no longer on them.

"Stay put while I draw the spell in the sand." The storm starts brewing out in the ocean as I carve the spells needed into the wet sand.

The clouds brew closer and closer at an accelerated pace, and the tide keeps coming nearer than I would like, but as the lightning begins to crack and the wind begins to blow, I cast this spell.

I open my eyes, and I see the second world his mind has created: infinite blackness with an overhead lamp, chord extending up into the forever.

"Derek!" I shout, looking around and around until he finally appears. "Ah, there you are."

"Doctor-" he tries to say, folding his arms, "I don't think-"

"No, Derek," I try to comfort him, "This is fine, I do my best work in later levels."

I reach into my pocket and pull out some chalk. I lean over and start sketching out the spell needed. I start drawing closer and closer to the darkness, realizing it's a fog, that moves along with my hand. It's cold and lifeless, but alive nonetheless.

"Doctor-" he goes on again, "I *really* don't think this is a good idea."

"It's fine, this is normal," I tell him. The fog begins to pulsate, swirling around as I cast this spell.

This construct looks like a forest, moon in the sky and overcast all over. The fog is intense, I can barely see the world, but the moon stares down at me, like a single eye watching us all in the night.

"Derek!" I shout, calling for my patient.

"Doctor," he calls out behind me. I go to look, and he looks happy and comfortable. His clothes are clean, like a wealthy young person he should be.

"Doctor-" I hear him say, but his lips don't move. The voice is weary, scared even. I look around and see another Derek behind me, but he sad, scared, dressed in poor clothes and missing all his fingers.

"Oh, Derek," I try to sympathize with, "Your disorders are beginning to manifest in extreme ways.

"It's normal to- for it to be like this, but we must go deeper." I rest my hand on the ground, forcing the magic here with my will and all three of us go one more level of the mind deeper.

"Doctor!" My blood curdles at the cries of the night, "Doctor Webber!"

The world is- unnatural. The dimensions we occupy are many but discombobulated. I feel like I'm floating, sliding through planes of existence, but this is where I must start working.

I begin to speak to the world, and feel it respond; it resists but begins to organize. I begin to feel my body forming from my heart to my fingers. The floor grows around my feet, and I hear the blood-curdling cries of a scared man, a broken man.

I open my eyes, seeing this world organize before me. I see my patient, hung and strung on a wall; pinned open akin to a newborn pig on display at a hospital. I stare at him, a living corpse soon to die.

"Help me," he whispers. A larger beast comes into view, it's teeth long and slender curving around to be the surgical pins holding him open and organs inside.

Long legs like ten spiders begin to step out of the darkness, one after another. Its body comes into view, still and dead. I attempt to reach down to the ground, but something pierces my hands through and through.

I scream in pain, and something begins to move the air back and forth like unearthly breathing. "It wants to go deeper, Doctor- don't- don't let it."

Something spreads into my hands, forcing the magic to be cast.

‹‹⊙›

I've never seen a case this severe, nothing I couldn't handle, but this is overwhelming. But this one, the 5th world, seems tranquil; the eye of the storm.

"Derek?" I ask, looking for my patient. I find a chair with three short, centered legs. As I approach the chair, I look all around and see columns of clouds, creating a wall all around.

I walk over to the chair and see a small fetus, laying on the seat with a spider crawling circles around it. I draw the circles needed around them to escape, but the spider hops onto my hand. It bites down and I lose control of my hand as it presses down and the spell to go one deeper.

I feel like I've awoken from a deep sleep, as I come to, I feel the worms crawling in and out of my body, running through and under my skin as they please. I try to scratch to alleviate the feeling, but fingers have been sloppily removed.

I look up to try and find something for me to climb my way out and I see the monster holding up a lifeless exhibit of Derek's body, insides sprawled out and hanging.

"Derek!" I try to shout, but the worms are crawling through my throat.

"Perhaps," it's voice echoes inside my empty skull, "This *isn't* enough for *you*; you magicians tempt fate and now fate tempts back."

The legs bend with creaks like old, broken wood and its body lowers down until Derek's lifeless head is atop of mine; the stench is putrid. Slender, lengthy needles begin to dig deep into his rotting flesh and his lips begin to whisper the very last spell.

"Are you ready, Derek?" I say, entering the room.

"Yes, ma'am," he says, holding his arms tight, scratching his cheek. I look closely at his face as he scratches and a scar on his forehead splits open to reveal an eye staring deep within my soul.

I blink and rub my eyes, thinking it's been a long day of horrors.

"Let's begin."

"I- I don't think that's a good idea," he replies.

"I'm a professional, I'll walk you through each step," I assure him, seeing another eye in my peripheral staring back at me, but I shew it away. "Let's begin."

I place my hands atop of his and try to cast the spell with no avail. I flashback to memories I don't recall making.

"Let's begin," I say, walking into the room. I feel Deja Vu, but I proceed anyway.

"Hi, Doctor," Derek says, greeting me. He appears to have four eyes, but it's just me being tired.

A harrowing voice reverberates within my head, "*Welcome, Doctor.*"

Memoir of Human Colonization

Everyone thought it was going to be Mars first, but it was Venus. Sky machines keeping people afloat above the clouds during terraforming. After 50 years of Venus, it proved life on other worlds was viable. Sky machine after sky machine populated Venus, to this day, it's still the least populated.

Mars was next in the sight of humanity: first established colony began to build, build for the next thousand people. It only took a few months to build, but a year to populate. 10 years and 10,000 people later, that first colony wanted independence, the United Nations had no choice but to enforce its dominance by sending in an army.

The African Space Coalition established another colony, not too far from the original focusing on agriculture to create a political and economical edge. No skirmish thus far, though.

After another long and grueling 10 years of unexpected famine, lack of supplies and care from the United Nations and African Space Coalition, the two colonies merged and establish a steel factory: iron from the soil and carbon filtered from the air. This boomed the economy, created all sorts of metal-related jobs. They built airtight skyscrapers and vehicles, but worst of all, guns.

What was left of UN-loyal soldiers fought against the combined colony and lost: 500 deaths total and a new nation was born named Collestri. China and Collestri struck a deal about population control. China sent tens or hundreds of thousands of people at a time in a year to Collestri, driving a terraforming initiative and dropping 6 thermonuclear bombs on both poles; 4 on north, 2 on south.

The Chinese population colonized to the west, on the plateau that would soon become a beach. With the added genetic diversity and radiation, population began to be born with white hair. China kept sending more and more people, totaling 10 million people over the 30 years or so that the interplanetary deal lasted.

'China Town' as it became known, they peacefully split into a separate country, keeping about half the population that was China-loyal. Total Mars population: 10 million; Total Venus population: 3 million. Total Time: 100 years.

All the wealthy countries began shipping people out to mars by the millions, conquering new and exciting landscapes that had been created by the terraforming. Landscapes began to be rigorously transformed by wild flora introduced by colonizers, and it began to mutate into something new, creating the first wild forests on an extraterrestrial planet.

India was next to start shipping people over; after 50 years of careful planning, they shipped a quarter of their 1.5 billion in-border population on the largest space transport ever built. It was a mass exodus to the far side of the planet.

Venus was neglected, skyships started being starved of resources as resources became scarce on Earth. A terrorist group bombed the main thruster of city-zero, dropping the city to the surface; no survivors, 2,000 dead. Total time: 150 years.

The UN blazed into unknowns of the outer solar system, regardless of the help Venus so desperately needed. Tests on human survival on the moons of Jupiter were first, whilst the rest of the flying cities of Venus were internally retrofitted to recycle the thick atmosphere, storing all dangerous and extraneous gas into energy storage tanks.

Survival tests failed on the moons of Jupiter, and they failed to be feasible to continue. The US Military started construction on even more massive and powerful transports, saying they'll take humanity to Saturn. The campaign failed, but the transports proved useful for human travel between planets.

With help from China, Collestri was able to sell steel throughout the stars, stimulating the independent economy there. The UN became the largest buyer, funneling the metals to the sky cities of Venus, building even more terraformers to transform the landscape to its once ancient glory.

India on Mars began excavation, unable to find signs of ancient life. Total time: 200 years.

Humanity blazed further into Mars' surface after plenty of engineers were able to build the technology that was kept from them during UN Occupation. New resources and technologies were able to be put to good use, along with Cave exploration for further, safer habitation.

Venus atmosphere filtration reaches 10% complete. Older cities form a coalition to represent themselves in politics, but the UN ignores their pleas. This leads to internal conflict and more retrofitting of the sky cities into weapons, threatening war on newer, UN occupied cities. Stored chemicals from atmosphere filtration are basically used to threaten as explosives. Another terrorist attack brings down another sky city.

Testing on Jupiter's moons starts back up again, salvaging older equipment left there from previous tests. The improved technology proves habitation to be viable, leading to military outposts on several moons for experimentation. Aquatic life discovered to be absent from Europa.

China town and Collestri join forces to build the nation's first rocket, further leading to a transport of their own, allowing them to finally break free from planetary limits. Life on Mars has also greatly improved, leading to a financial class system with jobs breaking out of the norm of farming, cleaning, and engineering. Farming on the planet has dramatically diversified from China pouring resources in strengthening their interplanetary empire.

India's colony remains separate from the other two nations, building up their own farming and other infrastructure. The Elder Venus Coalition officially separates from the UN, with the latter having no way to enforce occupation.

Collestri has expanded 2-fold into the mainland, Chinatown expanding along the coast. Total population of Mars: 800 million. Venus: 3.5 million. Total Time: 300 years.

Surface colonization of Venus becomes viable via heavily reinforced habitats, built by martian steel. Martian steel became the most cost-effective building material for interplanetary projects. The first land Venus colony building was crafted via remote-driven robots as atmosphere filtering nears 20% completion.

Collestri separates into north and south countries, fueled by internal conflict, although none were injured. China town separates from the Chinese Empire and forms Huoxing country. Total Time: 375 years.

US Military continues blazing further out into the solar system, planting flags on every moon possible, running experiments, going as far as Saturn.

North Collestri exports steel in the transport to The Elder Venus Coalition to build and retrofit sky cities to bring them back to safety from the brink of collapse.

A dictator takes the power of South Collestri. The country goes through extreme legislative reforms. They build a railway across the planet to make contact with the Indian colony. After 15 years of tension, South Collestri invades North Collestri. 1,200 casualties in the primary invasion, war ensues, another 30,000 die.

Huoxing country joins forces with North Collestri to fight back. Word finally reaches earth and the full might of the US and UN Military put a swift end to the regime, revealing the awful monstrosities that were being conducted in secret.

The US begins occupying South Collestri shortly after, with an estranged border being enforced between the two nations. North Collestri takes possession of the railway, finally establishing trade between all the nations of Mars.

10 years pass and the US Military attempts the largest scale transport that was ever designed; not only to travel to the nearest star, but to travel indefinitely throughout the galaxy. Total Time: 400 years.

Venus atmosphere filtering reaches 40%, allowing the building of even more land habitats, but also forcing the sky cities to lower elevation while consuming more power and fuel.

The US Military after 50 years of construction finish this galactic starship, and they announce plans to build two more. Most of the land habitats on the surface of Venus were converted to store the massive amount of liquid chemicals from filtering the atmosphere as the storage became too heavy to store on the sky cities. Several probes reach Saturn and Uranus from the US. Total Time: 450 years.

The UN and the US jointly start on a project that will propel scientific study into the next century. The World Singularity Project will construct a black hole and accompanying space station as a trans-Neptunian object in an orbit beyond Pluto and Charon.

It took 50 years to build the necessary outposts to create an interplanetary 'railway' from Martian steel for a transport to travel that far into the solar system. Another 50 years to engineer the required gravity engines and to build the space station. It was a momentous occasion when the black hole finally collapsed in on itself and started a scientific revolution for the human race.

In this time, Venus' atmosphere was reduced by 70%, allowing people, for the first time, to walk the surface of the sister planet. Total Time: 500 years.

"That concludes that 500-year history block, class," I turn off the projector, "Class is dismissed, come back on Thursday."

The Men of Iron and Blood

"Do it!" I shout, defeated; my armor shredded and my weak body bloodied from battle, "End this!

"For both of us." he holds his sword at my chin, seeing the pathetic body I inhabit. He pushes it closer, hesitating for the killing blow before pulling it away.

"Why?" he asks, setting down on a large piece of rubble, resting his armor, "Why do all of this? The world is in shambles because of you; you've brought on the apocalypse."

"You're just like me, back then," I say, the cold wind blowing on my shriveled legs.

"Tell me!" he demands.

It started when I was young, a spriting man out of university. A candidate man was running for US office, he was elected after a long, grueling race. On the second day of office, he started nuclear war with the Soviets, effectively ending the world. With an unstoppable military, he marched on foreign shores and took what he wanted, brutally disposing of what he did not.

But before that, I was fresh out of university, a degree in special relativity. I thought I would be the one to invent faster than light travel; I was so close to a breakthrough. But as fate would have it, I was diagnosed with late-onset muscular degeneration. My steps faltered every day until I was bound to a wheelchair. The world ended and something struck my mind; a simple change in variables could unlock backward movement in the fourth dimension: Interchronal travel.

I fled to Soviet Ruska to continue my research, confident I could finally unlock the secrets of the universe. When I finally had my breakthrough, my body was too far gone to make the journey, so I created an exoskeleton that interfaced directly to my spinal column. It took years of constant research, development, and sleepless nights to finish the technology. But when it was finished, I was ready to develop my world's time machine; a gun and a compilation of all my research in hand, I was ready to reshape the past like a god.

I finally started work on the interchronal travel machine; it took many more years to create the machine, even more to figure out the math to reach the destination I needed to go. I needed exotic fuels and energy fields to create a fourth-dimensional bridge between the two points in space-time.

I created another volume of condensed research and bullet with that terrible man's name and time of creation etched into the full copper jacketed lead. I secured myself inside the machine and engaged the trigger to send me back. The journey was beyond human description and comprehension. The intense energies merged my body with my suit, melding man and machine. But it was done: I had traveled the greater beyond back to the exact moment I had defined. I traveled to an abandoned building parallel to a political rally of that terrible man.

I readied the bullet, aimed, and fired, killing him instantly. The crowd went into disarray at the scene. The machine needed time to recharge, so I was stranded for the time being. Days later of waiting for the machine to come back into commission, I had met you, an officer searching for the one who fired the bullet. My arrest was inexorable.

They brought me in for murder, while you assessed my machines. You alone kept my volumes of research while I was tried for murder, and imprisoned.

It's when we first met when it began, our rivalry. I was well aware of your academic achievements, and I found it so peculiar that you so specifically assassinated the presidential candidate with a suit of armor and a bullet marked with a future date.

I too was an academic, studying something very similar before I joined a police force. The books that were on the scene I had taken for myself to decode their secrets. Before I had, you rebelled against the law, broke from our highest security prison and brought upon us the nuclear apocalypse yourself. Secretly I decode the future's knowledge as you committed genocide on the human race.

It took almost a decade to build the two machines described in your research volumes, but I believed it was too late; too much damage had been done by you. I decided I could stop you and your reign of terror to put an end to any more suffering, so I developed a new weapon that could stop you. One of my own design from the exotic materials you discovered: a sword that altered the strong nuclear forces holding together atomic nuclei.

My first mission was to destroy your interchronal travel machine and then you. And then I challenged you and our battle was legendary; the clash of two titans battling for the fate of the world. Steel against steel, wits versus wits; last light of good versus the reigning evil.

"And here we find each other, you at the end of my sword," I say to him, readying my sword against his frail flesh-merged-steel.

"So do it," he replies, "We both know the truth now; you know I won't stop, so end this for both of us!"

I swing my mighty sword and cleave his half-steel-half-flesh armor in two. The blood splatters against the rubble and ending the reign of terror.

And that was that; I dismantled the sword into fuel for the interchronal machine and traveled time to do what he couldn't: save the world. I knew the math, I knew the science, and I knew the exact point in space-time he traveled to. All I need to do is make the sacrifice he couldn't and end the terror from his world, the two coexisting instances of the man of iron and blood, and accept the consequences of murder.

And I did, the suit that interfaced with my body merged into my flesh during the travel, just as his. Just as he said, the trip was beyond description and comprehension, but I arrived moments before him. All I needed to do was disrupt his arrival to stop him. I place my machine where he would arrive.

He arrived on time, disrupted his arrival and killing him instantly and destroying the two machines. My left hand was untouched by the merging of flesh and metal, just enough to fire my old gun to kill the target. The police came when a giant suit of armor fired a shot to kill.

I willingly turned myself in, brought face to face with this past version of myself.

"Who are you?" he asks.

"I'm you," I reply, "From 30 years in the future."

"Okay, prove it to me."

"On the scene where you found me, you'll find the DNA of a scholar with a degree in physics-"

"He's been apprehended too."

"Where I'm from, *he* assassinated the presidential candidate, ruling in his own reign of terror."

"Really? You expect me to believe it?" I recount the last conversation we had to him, expounding on the nature of my arrival.

"This is all a tall tale," he folds his arms, leaning back in his chair and eyeing me up and down, "But between the gun, the bullet, *and* the two matching sets of DNA, it's a reliable explanation."

"So what will you do with us?"

"I've had the best scholars at hand reviewing these books you were found with-"

"They should be destroyed, I only brought them as proof of my story."

"You have burdened me with a unique purpose! Telling me all this; return to where you came from and I will ensure, *personally*, that this future doesn't come to pass."

They let me out, and the finest of scholars had built the interchronal machine once more, allowing me to return to the two worlds wrought by destruction, to rebuild them from the ashes of the dead and the rubble that now litters their worlds. The second trip was as magnificent as the first, melding the armor further into my body. We are the men of iron and blood, but I *must* be better than him to save the futures we created.

⊷●⊶

My Life as a Vampire

A Sequel to Grandpa's Old Shed

"Sarah!" Julie cries out to me, "Can you take me to school?"

Linda and Christopher must both be out doing their business. "Do you want to walk?" I shout out to the downstairs. I stand up and start applying my sunscreen. I hear footsteps run up the stairs, thinking it's Jule.

"I'm assuming *you* want to walk," she replies.

I smile and look down at my feet, thinking I might've forgotten my shoes downstairs. "Oh, you know me," I tell her, "I'm guessing Tina and Lila wanted to sleep in today?"

"Oh, you," she laughs. I pick up my umbrella and we walk down the stairs one after another. When we get to the door, I pat myself down for the keys and a cellphone I'm supposed to give to Jule for the day.

"Dad said I get the phone today, right?" she asks, while I search my mini-purse for it.

"Yeah, he just," I pause, fishing it out, "Wanted me to hold on for it for the night." I hand her the phone and we go on our way.

"You wore enough sunscreen, right?" she asks, "Or the right sunscreen, I should say. You have two different ones."

"Yeah, I wore the daylight one," I tell her, "I might have to go to the store after we get to school."

We continue on our way to her high school, about a mile walk. The sun still has yet fully risen, so I can walk without an umbrella and fully enjoy the sunrise.

"Tina said you were kind of feeling excluded in the family," Jule tells me, but I interrupt her.

"Not this again. I feel fine," I reassure her.

"You're like a sister to all of us, Sarah," she continues.

"I appreciate that, but it's just something else," I reply.

She turns around and starts walking backward, "Then what is it."

"It's nothing," I say.

"It's not nothing, you literally just said it was something," she persists on me.

"Nothing you should be worried about." the sun starts peeking out, casting its rays on me. I feel the warmth for a moment before putting up my umbrella.

We finally arrive at the school, and I walk Jule to the front door, giving her a nice hug before she goes off into the unknown. Something instinctual gets my attention, and I look around for what's triggering it.

I see a young man staring right at me, with a subtle unrest look on his face. I stare back, presenting my dominance, right before one of his friends pulls him away into the crowd. There's a lot of smells in the crowd I picked up on, but not sure if any of them are his.

I hear the familiar motor of the family car pull up through the street, reminding me if there's anything I needed to do before they come home. They have me clean twice a week and occasionally teach me how to cook a particular meal. The girls also show me their homework so that I can have some sort of education.

I hear the car turn around the corner and I make my way downstairs, look around to see if anything is in order. I walk into the kitchen and start straightening things out as I hear them turn the nearest corner to the house.

The motor stops in the driveway and the keys jingling follow up to the door. "Sarah, we're home," I hear Linda call out. It took quite a while for Linda to warm up to me; it took years for her to make sure Christopher wasn't having romantic behavior with me, but she warmed up nonetheless.

"Hey, Linda!" I shout back, walk out to greet them, "I'm just straightening out the kitchen."

"Oh, thanks," she says, "Julie said you walked her to school, that was sweet of you."

"Yeah, I like to walk during the morning when the sun isn't so bad."

"Yeah, there's been this guy stalking-" Jule starts talking.

"There's been a what?" I fixate, ready to kill.

"It's nothing," she says, "I just wanted someone with me."

I walk up to her and hug her, "Why didn't you say anything?"

"I didn't want to worry you-"

I interrupt her, "I have the time to worry, Jule."

Tina and Lila come through the door with Christopher. "Hey, Sarah," he says, "Do you think you can cook tonight?"

"Yeah, that's fine," I tell him. I lean over to Jule and whisper to her ear, "I'll beat his ass if you want me too."

She breaks out laughing and we all walk inside. "Chris, what'd you want me to make for dinner?" I ask him.

He looks at Tina, "Tina, it's your turn to choose?"

"What do we have?" she asks.

Chris look through the pantry, "You want Mac & Cheese?"

Tina gets wide-eyed at the possibility of her favorite meal. "Oh, yes, please."

Chris tosses me the boxes, and I look at the back to remind me of the directions. "Okay, I think I can do this," I reply.

As we eat, everybody's pretty quiet, enjoying the meal, but Lila speaks up. "How come we never see you drink blood?"

"Lila!" her mom chastises, "That's not something we ask."

I chuckle, "Oh, it's fine. I just don't do it around you guys."

Lila speaks out again, "Where are your fangs?"

"Lila," Chris speaks up, as Lila whimpers in silence, "Enough."

"I really don't mind," I reply.

Chris replies, "It's just not polite, Sarah."

"How'd I do this time?" I ask.

"Hehe, great," Lila tells me, giggling.

Tina gives me a thumbs up, stuffing her mouth with food. "It's great, Sarah," Jule assures me, "Do you think you could take me again to school again tomorrow." Julie winks at me while her father is looking down at the food.

"Oh, uh," I try to obviously wink back, "Yeah, sure."

I walk Jule up to the front door of the school, and I notice that kid walking up to. His scent became stronger and stronger, but just as disgusting: some sort of bad cologne.

"She's as white as paper, and just as see-through," he says, walking up to us.

"Go away," Jule tells him.

"Yeah, Go away," I say, "I'd rather not hurt anyone."

"That's cute that you think you can hurt," he places his hand on my shoulder, "Me."

"Go inside, Jule," I tell her, "I'll handle him."

"I didn't want her anymore anyway," he says.

I start using some of my special abilities as a vampire and grow small claws from my fingernails. My pupils start to dilate and my vision gets sharp.

He runs his other hand through my hair and I grab his other arm, sinking my claws into it. He starts backing off in pain, but I don't let go. "Ow, ow, ow," he starts saying, as I press my fingers through his leather jacket and skin.

"Leave her, and I, alone," I command him as blood starts dripping from his arm.

"Okay, okay, okay," he submits, "okay, I get it, let go."

"Please," I remind him to say. I look back at Jule, seeing her smile in revenge of some sort.

"Please, please," he begs, falling to his knees. I finally let go, and he falls backwards on the concrete.

"Have a nice day at school Jule!" I remind her, as she turns through the doors.

"Oh my gosh, Sarah!" Julie shrieks, "Did you see that dirtbag's face?"

"Before or after I made him bleed?" I laugh back.

The sun finally sets below the horizon on our walk from her school. Not so suddenly for me, a metal bat swings out from bushes. I catch the bat and pull it from that boy's hands. I've been smelling him for the entire walk.

"You gave me ten stitches!" he shouts, jumping out from the bushes, think he can surprise me. He attempts to punch me, but I catch his fist all the same. He tries to pull away from my intense grip, but I start to squeeze.

"I was hoping that you'd take the ten-stitch hint, kid," I tell him, releasing my grip, "Get lost." he looks like a deer with a shotgun to his head, and one of his cronies pulls him along the way.

"That was great," Jule tells me, laughing. She grabs my hand and realizing that I've been tremoring since this morning. "Oh, no. Why are you shaking?"

"It's nothing," I reassure her, "It's just something that happens when I do the *cool* things."

"Are you sure?" she looks skeptical.

"Yes, I'm fine," I assure her again.

We make our way back home. I'm smelling some cupcakes, with real vanilla. "What are you smelling this time?" she asks, as I sniff the air.

"I'm not smelling anything," I lie.

She play-shoves me, "Yes, you are. Don't lie. Lying is a sin."

"Whatever, I'm not telling you," I persist.

"You should totally apply to be a bomb-sniffing person," she tells me. We make our way up the steps and I unlock the door, blasting my nose with the strong scent of cupcakes and frosting.

"Welcome home, girls," Linda greets us, "How was school?"

Julie snickers under her breath, "Fine."

Linda raises her eyebrows in disbelief, "did you turn in your homework?"

"Yes," she chuckles, looking at me as I laugh back.

"What's the inside secret?" Linda asks, walking up to give me a hug, "Anyways, I made cupcakes, but Sarah probably smelled it from a mile away."

Every other Saturday morning, Christopher takes me to a local hospital for a 'blood transfusion'. I frequently smell other vampires there other than myself, but they always seem to be a bad bunch. I place the blood pack tube in my mouth and try to savor the blood, not drinking it down all at once.

"You're the best one that comes in here," the nurse reminds me, "Most of the others are hooked on something else aside from *this*."

The blood reaches my tongue, and it's like an ocean wave beating down on me and washing over me at the same time. Slowly, I take one sip after another.

"How often do you get other people like this?" Christopher asks the nurse.

"Oh, we get them every night, mostly," he replies, washing his hands clean, "You're some of the few we get during the morning."

Before I know it, it's all gone. I lean forward and slip, grabbing the arm on the other chair. The nurse helps me to my feet and sets me back in the chair. It's an addiction that never satiates, never subsides. "Take your time, honey," he tells me, "Don't try to be tough."

"I know, I know," I say, "I just-"

After all my tremoring subsides, and my legs aren't jelly anymore, we walk out and make our way back home. We get into the car in silence, and I still manage to buckle the seat belt. "So, Sarah, if you're up to it," Christopher says, "Jule is going to a party if you wouldn't mind going with her."

"Yeah, sure, I'd love to," I tell him, rolling over towards the window to hold my stomach. The blood is starting to digest and gives me a second wave of symptoms.

"Thanks, I'd appreciate that."

Jule and I walk through the night to her party she's supposed to go to. "Okay, so," she says, "We're not going to my friend's house, we're going out."

"What do you mean?" I ask.

"The party is just at a, uh," she replies, "club."

"A club?" I ask, reminding myself what a club is.

"Yeah, it'll be totally rad," she tells me, "Just, uh, don't tell dad." she turns around and starts walking backward, and pulls out two ID cards.

"Boom! Fake IDs," she says.

"Why do we need fake IDs?" I ask.

"Because you need to be eighteen to go into a club," she replies, "But all my friends are going to be there, so it'll be totes safe,"

"Okay?" I trail off, "I'm trusting that you know what you're doing."

"Yeah, totally," she says, turning back around and grabbing my arm.

I look up at the sky, not being able to see the stars as I used to at Abe's. There are lots of trees in the neighborhood; big, over-looming trees. Autumn is so much more enjoyable, being able to jump through the leaves with the kids, being able to cozy up during the winter.

We go past the school and further into the city, where I don't know the map, but I follow Jule anyways down the street and around the corner. The street is dirty and the sidewalks cracked with gum all around, a far cry from Christopher and Linda's.

She grabs my hand and leads me to the front door where we're greeted by a large man in a black suit with no tie. "You guys got ID?" he asks us.

"Oh right!" I say, pulling out my own ID, "Here you go."

Jule pulls out her fake one, but the guy still passes it on and lets us inside. The rank smell oozes out the door as it opens. I smell at least fifty people sweating, breathing and body odor, and chemicals I've never smelled before. It's all too much, and I start gagging as we walk through the door.

"You okay," she asks.

"Yeah," I manage to say before my nose starts to get used to all the smells, "It's just a lot."

The music is slow but loud, and people are just waving lighters around above their heads to the guitar notes. Jule pulls me through the crowd to a bar full of empty seats.

"Uh, one water please for my friend-"

"One whiskey for me," I ask the man behind the counter. Whiskey was Abe's drink of choice for the weekends, he would always share.

"Going hard tonight, ma'am?" he says, "ID?"

"But I showed the man at the door," I reply.

"Yeah, to get in," he explains, "You need to be twenty-one for alcohol."

I pull out my ID and he looks at it while pouring the brown liquid. The smell already brings me back by numbing my sense of smell. I pick up the drink and sip lightly, reminiscing on the memories.

"I'll pay for the lady," I hear somebody say, walking up behind me.

"Good, because I think it's the lady's first time at a bar," the man replies. I look behind me to see who it is, and I smell the faint scent of a vampire. He motions the man away and leans over to my ear as I sip my drink.

"You're a vampire," he whispers, leaning back to his seat, "Nice to make your acquaintance."

"Hi, uh," I freeze. This is the first time I've met a vampire since Christopher took me in.

"Don't worry, I'm one of the nice ones, like you," he tells me. Jule tugs on my shirt and winks very strongly.

"What does that mean, Jule?" I ask.

"I'm going to go with my friends," she says.

"No, I'm supposed to watch over you-"

"Then come with me!" she shouts as the song changes to a faster-paced one.

"But I'm talking to someone!" I shout back. She blows a kiss with her hand and walks off into the crowd, beginning to dance.

"Kids, right?" the man says.

"You're a vampire too-"

"Not so loud," he cuts me off, "People listen, but yes."

"I mean, that's quite the introduction," I say.

"I haven't met a decent one of you in a while, so you caught my eye."

I take another sip of the whiskey and collect my thoughts, what questions I want to ask another vampire. "So, whiskey, huh?" he asks, trying to make small talk.

"Yeah, my caretaker used to share with me," I tell him, "He died many years ago."

"How old are you, really?"

"I was born 1964, but I don't remember much," I tell him.

"What kind of vampire are you?"

"I was a savage one for a lot of years."

"Mhn. I fought in World War I, y'know," he says. I can't seem to remember which war that was, so I disregard it. The music seems to get even louder with all the other people now jumping up and down out of sync.

"So, uh," I try to think, "How's your day going?"

He laughs and takes a sip of his drink. "You're pretty cool, what's your name?" he asks me.

We walk out of that place, with a new phone number in my hand. It's late, and Linda is probably going to be more angry with Christopher this time. Jule and I have some residual smells from the place, I keep smelling some bad chemicals off of both of us I can't identify.

"Jule, breathe on me," I tell her. She rolls her eyes at me and continues to let a breath in my direction, which I don't smell any of those chemicals. "Sorry, I just don't want Linda to get too mad."

"So, you look like you have a boyfriend now, Sarah-"

"He's just someone I was talking-"

"You," she trails, "Have a boyfriend now. I saw him give you a phone number."

I laugh along side her, "Is that what constitutes a boyfriend nowadays?"

We make our way passed the school, with Jule occasionally skipping along and dancing from the music in her head. My nose is pretty numbed by the whiskey I had, but I can still make out the familiar smells on the way home.

We walk up the steps and I unlock the door. I see Linda in the dining room with a plate of pancakes, bringing me back to the days when all the girls were younger and Julie would demand pancakes at odd hours of the day, and Linda just couldn't say no to her little girl.

"Pancakes?" I ask.

"You were drinking again?" Linda asks me back, noticing I didn't smell the pancakes up the block.

"Yeah," I explain, with Jule winking very obviously at me, "they had some at the party, thought I'd help myself."

"You didn't share with the kids, did you?" she looks up at me.

"No, of course not," I reply.

"Mom, Sarah got a phone number from someone," she *spills the beans*, so to say.

"Oh, really? I didn't know you were up for dating now. I want to meet him," she demands.

"He's another vampire," I explain, "I don't know, y'know?"

She gets up from her chair and walks over to us, wrapping her arms around the both of us and holding tight for multiple seconds before letting go.

She leans over to me, "Just don't use up all the rollover minutes."

Jule and I go upstairs to go to bed at the late-night hour. "Thanks for not ratting me out, Sarah," she whispers when we get to the top.

"Can't say the same," I tease her, poking her in the arm.

The others are rounded up around me, all on our hands and feet ready to pounce one anything that moves. Another one of them bumps into me, and we get into a rumble, pushing and shoving each other mindlessly before we've broken up by the master, standing up on two feet like those we hunt. The thirst is insatiable, the hunger never easing, but the master feeds us. I look up and see his face, the ringmaster who herds us throughout the night.

My eyes open, revealing the ceiling I've been staring at this whole time. I look around to see my bookshelf full of books and the vinyl-covered window filtering out the morning sunlight. All the familiar things of life now.

I swish my saliva around with my tongue, feeling my teeth and closing my hands into fists to feel my nails. My nightmares used to force my body into a reaction, but it's less and less now.

Someone knocks on the door, and it opens slowly, revealing Tina. "Breakfast is ready," she says, "Are you okay, sis?"

"Yeah, I'm fine Tina," I tell her, "Just a bad dream."

"Okay," she reluctantly says.

I get up and straighten out my pajamas, feeling the sun's warmth on my hands and fantasizing for a moment of the burning I used to avoid for my life.

"Come on!" Tina says, "you don't want breakfast to be cold, do you?"

"No, I don't," I reply, slowly coming back to reality. I finally snap out of it and make my way down the stairs. One step after another and I slip on almost the last step and land on my bum.

"You good?" Christopher asks.

"Yeah," I groan, "I'm good."

My sense of smell has come back and I start smelling eggs and toast on Lila's request. I keep seeing them, day after day, getting older, while I remain the same. I think that's what Linda was feeling last night; both of us having midlife crises.

I sit down at the table and start enjoying the scrambled eggs. "Jule told me you have a boyfriend-" Christopher says, as I start choking on my food, "You okay?"

"Not," I make out through me coughing out a lung, "Boyfriend."

I finally manage to stop coughing whilst everyone staring at me, chuckling.

"Totes boyfriend," Jule says, as I glare at her.

Linda chimes in, biting into her toast, "He's another vampire."

"Oh," Christopher remarks, "You call him yet?"

I cover my face and pick around the eggs with my fork as he laughs.

"I mean," I say, "The last vampire I talked with, I ended up nailing him to your wall, so I wouldn't say I'm eager to-"

"He's cute though," Jule interrupts me, "Looked rich, too."

I begin to feel my cheeks get warm as I blush and drop my fork. Somehow, we all break out laughing in hysteria.

I dial the phone number, waiting to press the final button to call. I can hear the girls with their ears pressed against the door, with Linda walking up the stairs.

I press down on the phone to call, and the longest three seconds of my life are spent waiting and wanting him to pick up. "Hello?" I hear his voice.

"Hi, I'm looking for Brandon," I say, rubbing my face, "From the bar the other night."

"Sarah?" she asks, with me confirming, "How have you been?"

"Good," I try and say something without pause, "Just- Uh, chilling." I hear the girls giggling giddy from the other side of the door, with Linda shooing them away.

He laughs on the other side of the phone, "Can I take you out to dinner, sometime?" the girls start making noises, and I can smell Linda by the door as well.

"Oh, uh," my brain doesn't want to formulate words as I'm trying to talk, "Sure?"

"How's tomorrow night?" he asks. My bedroom door bursts open, and Jule comes running up.

"I'll have to take her shopping, big boy," she commands, "But she'll make it: eight o'clock and don't be late." she presses the stop the call, and all the girls start jumping up and down in excitement with Linda laugh-crying in the background.

"Oh my gosh, Julie!" I shout.

"Oh, please," she tells me, "You were being gob-stopped, Sarah."

"I was not!" I retort, knowing full well that I was.

Linda and the girls took me night shopping at the nearest mall in the city. The girls would just pull me around from store to store, forcing me to try on clothes, but it was nice. I've haven't been on a big shopping trip like this since they took me in, making me get rid of most of the old clothes from Abe's.

When we got home from shopping, they put me through the rounds with the makeup, having to scrub my face twice to start over, once because Lila couldn't put the lipstick on right.

Seven-fifty-eight on the clock and Linda is spraying me with her fancy perfume, but she's used a little too much for my nose. "Linda?" I call out to her.

"Yes, dear?" she says, in the kitchen, washing her hands. I walk up to her and wrap my arms around her.

"I'm here if you need to talk," I tell her, "I'm technically ten years older than you."

"I know," she replies, patting my hand with hers.

Eight o'clock on the dot, the doorbell rings, but Christopher is there waiting with a UV flashlight in hand opening the door. The door swings open and I see and faintly smell Brandon.

I see Christopher tighten his grip on the baton light. "You must be this *Brandon* I was told about."

"Yes, You must be part of her host family," he replies, looking past him for me. I move into view, seeing the setting sun blocked by his large umbrella. "I was told by a young lady to be here at eight?"

I see the girls peeking through the railing on the stairs, and Brandon waving at them. "There's the lady of the hour," he says, looking up and down at me. I walk over to Christopher and take the baton.

"I'll be back at midnight," I tell him, placing the flashlight on the table by the window. I give him a hug and extend my umbrella to hide from the sun; Jule insisted that the sunscreen smelled too bad. Side by side, we walk down the steps and to the sidewalk, where a black strangely styled car awaits.

"You like it?" he asks.

"It's a far cry from Chris' and Linda's cars."

"I got it in 1950," he says, "Still original."

"That's pretty old,' I giggle.

"You're nervous," he tells me, opening the door for me, revealing the leather interior with red accents.

"I mean, the last vampire I talked to, I ended up staking."

"Well, sometimes, it's kill or be killed for us." I pull my dress down my legs and sit down. The door closes, and I smell the driver through my perfume.

The door opens on the other side and he sits down next to me. "You look great tonight," he compliments me.

"Thank you," I reply nervously, looking around at the luxury car.

He looks at me, and I look back at him. "You're not impressed," he says.

"I just, uh, don't know what's more than Christopher and Linda."

"You're host family," he says, "They seemed nice, how long have you been with them?"

I reminisce about the memories of the girls and Abe. "About eight years, and their grandfather for fifteen before that," I explain.

"I don't usually see vampires staying that long with a host family."

"It's not normal?" I ask.

"Mostly with younger vampires," he explains, "Or new vampires getting their bearings in the new nightlife. How long have you been a vampire?"

The car hits a bump and shakes the car. "I don't really know."

"Oh, that's right," he recalls our conversation from the bar, "Do you know who your ringmaster was?"

"My what?"

The car slides to a stop, "We've arrived," the driver tells us.

"You're ringmaster?" he asks, "They round up savage vampires to amass an army of sorts, to challenge other vampires."

"Oh, you'd have to ask the coroner."

He gets out and moments later reappear, opening my door for me. I get on my feet and I look around at the new environment. I see the big sign for the restaurant, something I can't read. "Fancy," I say, admiring the lights and clean walls.

"The best," he says, "When you're over a hundred years old, you afford the best. I rented a booth all the way in the back."

I grab ahold of his arm, and we walk together to the inside, being escorted by a man in a shiny black suit. It's full of the smell of roasted meat and strange alcohols; wine, I think. He leads us behind a curtain and a round, half-circle booth.

Then, something hits my nostrils: human blood. My hands start to shake as my body starts it's hunger.

"Are you alright?" he asks, sitting me down on the edge of the semicircle.

"I smell," I gather my bearings, "I smell blood, I can't be- I can't be around that."

"Oh," he waves his hand at the waiter waiting for us to sit down. I see him grab the two glass on the table and walk off behind the curtain.

My fingers start to curl in addiction, digging into the wood of the table. "Sarah," he reaches out, "Are you okay?"

"Yeah," I persist, "I'm just on the tail end of my two weeks." He rests his hand on my back as I collect myself.

"You feed every two weeks?" he asks, sitting down across the table.

"Is that too short," I take a deep breath in and out.

"I feed once a month," he explains. He motions for the new waitress, "Two specials, please."

"What's the special?" I ask, reaching for the water.

"It's chicken, is that okay?"

I take a big swig of the water in a very unladylike fashion. After catching my breath, I manage to say, "Yeah, that's fine."

He laughs at me a little. "You know, you're very different than other people I've taken out."

"Oh, how so?"

Twelve o' five on the clock, he walks me up the steps to the house. "We should do this again, Sarah, what do you think?"

"Yeah, yeah," I prepare myself for the barrage of the daughters, "Maybe I can have you over for dinner? At the house?"

"That'd be a first in eighty years," he chuckles.

I knock on the door, and it swings open before I can knock a third time. Jule stands there, ready to face an army. She grabs my arm and tries to pull, but I resist it.

"Sarah!" she shouts, "You're ruining my dominance move." I see Christopher and Linda sitting, eating for a late-night snack at the dinner table.

I swing my head, accidentally slapping my hair in Brandon's face and go along with her tugging. "Bye," I whisper, "I'll call-"

"She'll *call* you," Jule shouts, yanking me through the door.

"Bye-" I try to stay, waving my fingers at him as the door shuts.

"You're late," Christopher says, "I'd rather not beat his ass-" Linda punches him in the arm to shut him up. Jule keeps pulling me up and up the stairs. Tina and Lila peek out their shared bedroom door, giggling like little girls, but Jule drags me into her room.

"Jule," I laugh, I haven't seen her this excited in years. She pulls me and sits me down on her bed.

"Tell me *all* about it," she demands, crossing her legs on the bed.

"It was good-"

"I want *details*, Sarah," she insists. I hear Tina crawl up to the door, listening in.

"Well," I start, going on about my night.

Linda agreed to have Brandon over for dinner, and the girls *promised* to be on good behavior; Tina I believe, but Lila and Jule I don't, especially Jule.

I look out the window, the sun still shining from the sky. "Don't you think six o'clock was a little too early?" I ask aloud.

Christopher walks up behind me, "As the father figure here, I don't think so, if he wants to come, he'll think of a way to get here."

Clock in the kitchen reads five fifty-eight, and that nice car he has someone drive for him arrives. The door opens and the embroidered umbrella peeks out and expands. I try to get a better look at what he's wearing the umbrella is large and hiding him in the shadows.

He walks up the steps and Christopher tries to open the door, but I grab the handle and lightly shove him away since he's brandishing Abe's UV baton. He walks up to the door reaching out for the doorbell, and I see white gloves and a thick wool overcoat.

I open the door, carefully avoiding the sun rays to reach for his hand and bring him in. "Good afternoon," he says, "It's clear skies all day, Sarah. Your family is really wanting me to prove myself, aren't they?"

"Yeah," I exclaim, pulling him in. I reach out too far and some sun burns my hand. I pull back, pinching his hand.

"Good afternoon, Brandon," Christopher says.

"Hello, *Christopher*?" Brandon tries to recall his name from our date the other night.

They shake hands as he comes inside and collapses the umbrella. I take a good look at him and his thick wool jacket in the middle of autumn and white gloves.

"I apologize for the heavy clothes, but it's still sunny," he says.

Linda comes out of the kitchen with a dish full of that home-cooked pasta I like and the kids come running down the stairs, pushing through Julie who's been waiting at the top of the stairs.

"I hope you like pasta, Brandon," Linda says, before stopping to take a good look at him.

"I do, thank you," he replies, taking off his jacket, not knowing where to put it, "Um, can I place this somewhere."

"Just on the chair right there," Linda tells him.

He places it down and then stands next to me at the table. Jule finally makes her way to the table so we can all sit down. I'm surprised when I can't feel the chair, realizing it's been pulled out for me. We all sit down and Linda starts saying grace; I look over to Brandon who's looking around frantically, not knowing what to do. I laugh a little, followed my Lila, who's also staring at him.

"Amen," we all say in unison, with him saying it later out of sync.

The girls reach out for the food, and I prepare myself for the interrogation I've been told was going to happen. "So," Jule announces, "What are your intentions with my sister?"

"Oh, uh," she catches him off guard, "I suppose I don't have any at the moment."

"Mhmn," she mumbles, right before taking a bite of her servings.

"So," Linda breaks the silence, "You're a, uh, vampire as well?"

"Yes," he says, "I actually fought in World War I."

"Oh, really," she takes a bite of pasta, "That must've been a nightmare."

"Yeah, it was," he says. Jule winks at me, and Tina sees it and laughs. "I was actually turned into a vampire halfway through the war."

Christopher chimes in the interrogation, "So the age difference between you two doesn't bother you?"

"Uh sixty, seventy years, no," he says, "Age sort of, um, disappears for us- us vampires."

"I see."

"What do you do for a living?" Jule asks.

"I guess you could say I'm in retirement," he explains, "I had a small inheritance, and I worked nonstop for, like, fifty years."

"Hmn," Jule grunts.

"How's the food?" I ask him.

"It's good," he replies, "I haven't really had someone to make me a home-cooked meal for a very long time."

Lila and Tine start whispering over something embarrassing, so I wish they wouldn't talk. I look over to Brandon, who's smiling because I know he can hear it.

Lila finally bursts out, and my face turns red. "Can vampires have babies?" she asks. I spit out a little of my water, and Linda pinches her ear.

"Um," Brandon says, "I'm not too, um, sure about that."

The girls start laughing and Christopher chuckles a little bit. I just cover my face with both hands and look down at my food.

Jule's finally going to go to college this year; she got accepted into a high-end college with a few grants. Linda is deep down having a full swing mid-life crisis.

She makes her rounds of goodbyes at the train station. She gets to Brandon and I and we give a nice group hug. "I'll have someone pick you up at each of your stops," Brandon tells her,

"That's very sweet of you, but-" Jule says.

"I insist."

Linda walks up and whispers into Brandon's ear, "You don't have to do all this, I'm it's costing way too much-"

Brandon replies with a rough estimate of how much money he has, and Linda replies simply with, "Oh."

Jule kisses her sisters and walks up the steps inside the train cart. We all wave goodbye, and Linda's crying a little in Christopher's arms. We'll see her for Christmas, I suppose.

Obadiah's Legend

The Legend Continues

⊷⊙⊶

And what then happened to Obadiah?

Thus the legend continues; some say the desert resurrected him from that cavern's grave he rested in.

The Grave of Two Masters?

Yes; the catacombs of the ancients. Are you ready?

I am.

⊷⊙⊶

The breath of life once again enters my bosom and I awake from the slumber of death's embrace. *Begone Reaper*, I hear a familiar voice whisper to my soul.

I open my eyes to see the darkness of the catacombs surrounding me. My body aches as if I had a mountain resting on me. I see as I look, rubble burying me.

I bring my hands together to cast a spell to remove the rubble from around me. "Zemerin!" I cast, to no avail. I look down to only see one of my hands holding the position.

I look to my left to see if my arm is still buried, but I find it missing, with runes burned into the stub. I start to remove the rubble with my single hand, rock by rock. Eventually, I am free. I see the burnt remains of Malik's bones, embedded into the molten stone now solidified into the wall.

"I suppose he is really dead this time," I tell myself. The catacombs are filled with the remains of the ancients, but they exist below the desert.

"You've awoken." I hear that familiar voice.

"Hakim!" I call out, "Show yourself."

I raise my finger and summon a flame to light the catacombs, looking for the source of his voice. I see him, in the flesh, standing in the entrance.

"Obadiah," he speaks, "You definitely killed him." he begins to laugh a little and walks into the light.

"With help from you," I reply, looking at the catacombs in the light.

"Come," he motions for me, "I know the way to the surface."

We walk together in the red flame illuminating the caverns. He guides me in the flesh as he guided me in the spirit.

"You are able to become astral?" I ask, looking at the decaying bones of the ancients.

"Yes, I can."

"That's a very advanced technique."

"Yes, it is," he responds.

I stop and say, "Who are you really?"

"You aren't some old man," I persist, "Not a single soul at my monastery could become an astral being."

"It's an ancient technique-"

"You are an ancient man to match," I say, "And what of my resurrection?"

He motions I keep walking, but I remain steadfast. "I am," he pauses, "An immortal being from long ago."

He motions again for us to resume our travels through the catacombs, and I walk beside him. We twist and turn, walk up sets of steps until he stops me. I raise my finger to see a stone wall, barren from the last resting place of a body.

"Here is the entrance," he points to the barren wall.

"This is a wall, Hakim," I retort back to him.

"The catacombs exist separate from the desert," he speaks, "You must open a doorway."

"This is too advanced," I reply, "Ancient, forbidden spells such as this are impossible to cast."

"Then create a new spell," he commands.

"My abilities are none with a single hand."

"No," he corrects me, "Your abilities are what you believe them to be."

"No," I persist, "Without it, I am unable to control the flow-"

"No, Obadiah," he chastises me, pressing his finger into my bosom, "The flow is controlled by your heart!"

"We'd be here for ages before I could create something that advanced!" I shout, realizing Hakim was never here and I was alone in this cavern. I float this flame around me as I press my hand against the earthy wall. My heart beats and I yearn for my settlement hidden in the desert.

Suddenly I find myself standing beside a closed wooden door, weathered from time. I look to see a bustling city with asses and camels walking about the street, not too asimilar to my old settlement. I remove my hand from the door and stumble down the street. I use my remaining hand to tie my garment around my stump.

I approach a humble merchant resting in the shade of his tent. "Where is the city hidden in the desert?" I request of him.

He raises his head to look upon me, "The city hidden in the desert is no longer hidden."

I begin my journey once again, wandering through the city. I hold my hand out to read the ley lines of this city, but I don't recognize the patterns. A foolish child walks up to me and raises his finger to me.

"Look, an invalid," he scowls, but I turn the other cheek and continue on my journey throughout this estranged city. I approach a clearing between buildings and see a tower unlike I've ever seen. It was an exquisite green, shimmering in the harsh sunlight with an orchestra of colors on the tip.

"What is that building?" I pull someone close, pointing at the magnificent tower.

"Obadiah's tower," he replies, "It was built to commemorate the hero and act as a monastery to train new masters." I release my grip and storm off beyond the reaches of the city into the desert.

The sun beats me down into the desert sand. "Hakim!" I cry out. I drive my thumb into my palm and bleed.

I let the blood flow into the soil and cast a summoning spell, a forbidden cast to summon a vision to carry me away to no avail.

I travel further into this city, approaching the iridescent tower off in the distance. The townspeople scowl at me as I travel by, not knowing of me.

"Are you lost, invalid?" a man scowls at me.

I rush up to the man, holding him to the wall with my lonesome arm and glare deep down in his eyes, "Where in the name of the gods am I? Where is the hidden city?!" He shoves me away, going on his merry way. My vision wavers as I go on, my step falters and I fall to the ground without breath.

"Hakim," I whisper to the universe, calling for his soul.

When I open my eyes I find myself inside the tower, being prised through.

"Your arm," I hear a voice speak to me, "How did you lose it-"

"Where is the hidden city?" I persistently ask.

"The hidden city?" He responds, coming into my vision. My eyes clear and I see him plainly, "I know not of a hidden city.

"What is your name, traveler?" he asks of me.

"I'm who they call Obadiah."

"Obadiah? I recount the hero who saved the desert to be Obadiah, you bear his name."

"What became of this Obadiah?"

"He fought a corrupt king, and they disappeared beneath the desert."

I seize him by his garment and pull him down, "How long ago?"

"80 years ago this happened," he tells, "It is recounted in our library."

"You've been struck with a fever, my friend," the master says to me, keeping me from going back on my travels, "Rest."

"Nay," my legs are weary and my heart is heavy, but he persists on holding me against this place. "I search for one named Hakim."

"Halt your search, patron of the desert," he rests beside me, "Allow yourself to heal; blood stains your garments."

And thus he stayed, allowing his appendage to heal, though no soul knew he, the one who saved the kingdom and defeated the corrupted king.

I pull another book from this library of magic, books of faraway lands. I set the book back on the shelf, unable to find anything pertaining to the flow of magic of lost limbs.

"Show yourself, Hakim!" I grit my teeth. I look to see Hakim placing a book back on the shelf. He looks upon me.

"You'll never find what you're looking for here," he says, brushing his hands against the books, "Nothing here I couldn't've taught you."

"Hakim-"

"Consorting with blood magic," he continues, "That's dangerous, Obadiah."

"I'm missing an arm!" I shout.

"It's not about that," he walks over to me, lifting my garments to see the healing wound, "The runes held up well." I shove his hand away. He looks up at me, "What do you want me to do, Obadiah? You must learn again!"

I grab his garments, glaring deeply into his old eyes, 'O how much they've seen, realizing he's not here; he was never here walking these halls.

"Are you enjoying our library?" the head master asks me.

"I was once a great master of my own right," I confess to him, "I even helped colonize the desert."

"What happened?"

"I fought a corrupted Master, fallen from grace."

"What monastery did you learn in?" he brushes the books with his hands, brushing the dust from them.

"*Janubii,*" I tell him.

"That monastery fell a long time ago," he reminds me.

"So did I."

The master and I sit across from each other, "I've taught someone with your particular disability before.

"It's like-

"A raging river, and we must-

"We as practitioners, must-

As we synchronize, we say, "control our portion of the river."

"You've lost your ability to control it, *you must learn again*," I hear Hakim's voice speak through him, "You must carve your own way."

We meditate and I try to carry myself into a vision. I open my eyes to find myself in a skyscape, some astral plane of existence. I open my mind's eye and see myself befront me; the very flow of life originating from my bosom, flowing out like the raging river. The construct grows and consumes me, leaving in a void of blackness alone.

I stand to my feet and I hear footsteps echoing, I look to see behind to find no one. The footstep persists echoing and I notice my two hands. When I raise my head, the corrupted King rushes me and palms my chest, tearing away my arm.

"Nothing I couldn't've taught you," the voice Abd al Hakim speaks, "Get up!"

I grudge to my feet, "Teach me, Hakim!" A storm brews, thunder sings and lightning dances violently. It strikes befront me, summoning the personage of Hakim.

"No," he whispers, striking me down into the void. I see the storm as I fall into the abyss. When I strike the ground, the storm arrives to light the darkness.

I come face to face with myself, young and spriting, before he fades away in the wind. Everything falls silent and I'm befront Hakim. I fall to my knees and reach out for him with my single hand. "Teach me," I beg of him.

"No," he whispers, "Not yet."

My mind's eye closes and my worldly eyes open to find myself in the iridescent tower alone.

The head master of this tower approaches me, bringing me some tea. "Your arm is healing well," he sits beside me, "May I see?"

I reach and untie the garments to reveal the wound. "These markings are mysterious, where do they originate?"

I set the tea dish down, "Who am I to know?" I tie up the garments once again to cover the shame. "I'm going into town."

"Will you bring back a cabbage?" he asks.

"If I decide to return." I continue on my way to the outside. The streets are busy as they always are; I remember the simpler times, but 'o how time changes the world, yet I remain the same tragic husk of the great man I used to be.

I wander the streets, looking for something familiar that I had built with my own hands. But I'm stopped by a young man, sword in hand.

"Show us some magic, you invalid," he says to me as a few others surround me.

"Leave me be," I try to move, but they shove me back. I look up to see Hakim standing, spectating from a crate.

"Show us something!" he draws his sword, posing to fight.

I crouch and sweep his legs away from him. A blade swings down, skimming my face and I rush to my feet, kicking him against a wall. The third readies his fists against mine. He swings his arm, I catch it underneath in the hollow of my shoulder, breaking the young man's limb before kicking him away.

I look back up to find a child standing on the crate to watch the fight, but I go my way to the vendor who sells the vegetables the head master prefers.

"Ah, *Samat!*" he greets me, "What will it be today?"

"A cabbage," I tell him, placing some money in his hand and picking up the cabbage. He cheers me away as I go back to the tower, passing by the young men who attempted to attack me.

I look upon the desert from the top of this tower, a monument to the arts standing tall above everything for as much as the eye can see. The desert is a mystery, ever-changing.

"I too admire the landscapes from up above."

"I once fought a powerful king, he opened the ground beneath us and I saw a glimpse of the Ancient's catacombs."

"There are stories of that day," he tells me, "It is recounted in the library."

"I'm no longer that man."

"No, Obadiah," he motions that I follow, but I stay, looking out into the desert, "Change is inexorable."

"I thought I could never fall from grace, look at me now."

He rests his hand on my shoulder and as I look at him, I see Hakim. "Why am I haunted so?" I ask him. He motions his hand and summons a flame.

"I brought you from the dead, and for what?" he retorts, "Not for you to sulk!"

"I died a hero!" I shout at him, "You resurrected a hollow husk!"

"I wanted the hero to shine once more in a time of need!" He palms my chest, releasing the flames all around, casting me in a vision of the future where I sense a dark presence come over me, "A dark force grows off beyond the horizon."

The vision fades as I fall to the ground, "Why couldn't you have found another champion?"

"None other could do," he tells me, "Even with your condition."

And thus, Obadiah left the tower and traveled hence into the desert. He traveled until the tower left the horizon to the south. He found the dune that rose above all else, and in three days' time, he reached the summit where the cold wind blows on the skin; where the radiant sun burns down.

I recall a symbol I had seen in a dream, perhaps originating from books from the library, that carried me into the unknown, and trace it on the sand befront me. I whisper the spell, imbuing its power in my hand and thrust it down in the sand.

A great serpent materializes, slithering and crawling the likeness of the markings in the sand. I whisper to it, "Let your power flow through me, so I may defeat evil. My soul be thine."

The great serpent comes hither and creeps up my arm and perches on my body. I stand to my feet, renewed in power from the gracious, life-giving desert and march back to the tower.

"You've returned, Obadiah," the head master greets me, "I had thought you left for good."

"Teach me the ways," I beg, kneeling before him.

Hakim's voice speaks through him, "You've been humbled, Obadiah. I shall."

Obadiah trained in the new ways, forgetting what he was taught in his days over 80 years prior. He relearned all he new in preparation for the dark presence looming in the future.

"Your sword, Master Obadiah," head master Amare hands me a finely crafted blade. I gratefully accept and slide it on my hip, "May you fight your battles bravely."

I stand to my feet and the serpent raises its head to where I need to go. I bow to my master and head on my way. I find myself walking through the hall of mirrors and the reflection is not my own, but of Abd al Hakim, the servant of the wise.

"You're not done learning," he says to me.

"I've learned all I will here, I must go learn the rest on my own."

"Then go, the voice of that great serpent will guide you." the last mirror leaves view and I'm left alone as I travel into the desert. The city is gone behind me and the great expanse of sand and sun is ahead. The great serpent goes from me and guides me through the harsh reality and journey.

He traveled by the great serpent's guide for weeks before it stopped at an oasis, It drank the water thereof and carved a rune into the sand in which Obadiah took a stone and etched it into the blade, imbuing it with certain power.

I look up from the oasis and see a storm brewing off in the distance, feeling the evil contained within. I know this is my destination, destiny's fate for me. The great serpent creeps back on me as we resume our travels.

And what happened next?

Obadiah fought a great battle, saving the desert once more.

                        Amazing.

Aye, but the legend is yet to be finished.

⇤⊙⇥

Titan, The Necromancer

"I'm so sorry," I vaguely hear my mother say to somebody who isn't relevant, "He's *special*, he doesn't understand..."

I see a bird, laying on the ground. A small one, possibly a newborn who could not fly. My friends begin whispering a cacophony of darkness into my ears. They whisper dark magic to me, but I often ignore them.

My focus begins to change from the world to the bird as the world tunnels into darkness. *Rise- tell it to rise*, my friend tells me. "*Rise,*" I say, and the bird begins to twitch, but my focus is interrupted my mother snatching me up into her arms.

"Stay away from that!" she shouts as the bird flaps it's wings and flies away.

"Tell that boy to stay away from my family!" the irrelevancy says, "He's evil, just like his father!"

I open my eyes back to reality from the dreamfulness of my slumber. The sun shines and the wind blows as it always does. Today is another day in which I follow my father's craft. I get to my feet and get dressed, readying myself for class.

I open the door ready to everyday discomforts. My friends start their whispering, telling me all kinds of things. They ridicule the sloppiness of the uniforms of people around me, telling me that I've done well to keep myself presentable, but someone tells me otherwise.

I walk into my class, moments before we're ready to start. I see a grimoire sitting befront my seat. My friends tell me not to sit down, it's a prank. "Devil man!" I hear, "Devil man!"

I take the book and bring to the front desk, the moment I touch it, I hear the cacophony in my ears saying crude things, but it ceases when the book is no longer in my grasp. *Devil man, evil man.*

The teacher walks in and I go to my seat, ready to learn today's lesson on the magic arts.

The sun shines and the wind blows on my daily stroll about the city to try and stay healthy amidst my studies. My friends always join me, whispering all their thoughts in disarray. I step past a library, and my friends tell me to go inside, but I keep walking to their dismay. But one of them stays behind longing for me to return by the door.

I return to class, and attend to the readings I'm assigned. My instructor has given me special instructions to be mindful of what I study. "I've been informed by your mother that you've had an affinity for necromancy," he tells me, "I'm forbidding you to practice such things at this grade level; you're to stick to the basics of the curriculum."

"Yes," I reply, distracted by my missing voice, "Where did he go?"

He snaps around trying to recapture my attention, "Did you hear me?"

"Yes," I tell him, "No necromancy, I understand." I leave to go look for my missing friend, and in my travels, I find myself back at the library to see him waiting patiently at the door. The messy thoughts become loud as I walk up to the door.

"Your destiny lies within," I make him out to say, "without me." shivers runs deep within my spine, but I take the steps up as he leads me and the rest of my friends inside. The door shuts and he falls silent to the dismay of the shamble of voices.

"Good evening, How can I help you?" I look to see a dark woman, sorting through some books. Books as far as the walls tend to reach all organized in neat little shelves.

"I was wondering if you have grimoires here," I ask, mesmerized by the library.

"Yes," she answers me, "Of what variety are you looking for?"

"Necrotics," I look up at her, she looks back with an estranged look on her face.

"We do, I'll show you to them." she leads me through the maze and my friends scatter about, scanning through all the glorious books. They mumble and grumble at what they find and talk aloud in the silence. She motions to the collection of books, and I see an edition marked '1'. I slide it out and take it to a nook lying just behind the shelf

"Thank you," I tell her, going off on my own. My friends go off about the library, searching and reading to me the books of magic this building contains.

I see them run amuck, taking books and reading them to me as I listen to them all read to me. The sun sets and the dark woman approaches me. "Unfortunately, it's time to shut the doors for the day," she tells me, as I close the grimoire, "We'll open back up at the crack of dawn." I walk with her back to the shelf and I place the book back on the shelf whence I took it from.

I find myself walking down the halls of this school, ready to make the trek back to the library. *WACK!* A book rams into the back of my head. I look to see some others rallying against me.

"I heard this nerd went to the library," someone ridicules me, "like he doesn't get enough here."

They walk off through another path and I'm left with my friends once more as I walk this path. The walls clear out and the sun shines and the wind blows. Their voices tell me which way I should go, but they never agree. I find myself once again wandering past the library where he sits by the door, beckoning me inside.

And for a moment they all say, "We need more." they push me in resistance to the door. I walk inside and the dark woman waves at me, giving me a warm feeling inside.

"Good afternoon," She says to me, "Back for more?"

"Yes, ma'am," I reply, going off to read the next grimoire in the collection.

I pull it off the shelf and see the leather cover and metal corners. I go to my nook behind the shelf and begin to read whilst my friends read their own discords. We read until the sun sets and the library closes for the night.

I come back the next day, and the next. I see my friend by the door whither away as he waits for eternity for something. Slowly my friends come together and their voice forms a symphony of knowledge feeding into my brain.

School falls to the wayside as I learn the knowledge of necromancers beyond the generations, learning to summon the dead. I pull out the last volume in this library, sealed away for the forbidden knowledge that lies withing, only being opened by those skilled enough to perform the complex ritual to open the lock.

"Miss?" I ask the librarian, "Do you mind if I take this one home?"

She looks over the desk to view the book I'm holding. My friends whisper to themselves doubts about my decision. "That's a rare volume," she tells me, "I expect you to bring it back tomorrow."

"Yes, ma'am," I gid, smiling back at her.

"You're quite the unconventional boy, but I'm glad you find joy in knowledge."

I turn tail and walk out the library, going to my dorm.

I set this final grimoire on the desk of my lone dorm, and draw a circle of chalk around it, placing a picked rose on the left and an egg on the right. I whisper a spell and green energies surround the book, and finally all my friends fall silent for the first time. The sounds of their voices no longer rings about my head and I hear nothing.

The metal lock flips open and the energies dissipate. I sit down in my chair and read in deafening silence, committing the spells and lessons to memory. The night goes on and I finish this last grimoire, closing it and locking the latch.

"What are you doing?" I hear my headmaster suddenly ask me in anger.

I turn around and try to hide the book behind me. "I was-"

"That's a forbidden volume!" he shouts, "I thought I told you not to practice that kind of magic!"

"I was only reading it, I haven't performed anything," I whisper like a scared mouse.

"I've put up with too much from you, give me the book!"

"It doesn't belong to me-"

"Damn right it doesn't!" he rushes me and steals the volume.

"No!" I reach out, but he's rushing away from me, "That belongs to the library!" I start running out after him, only to be knocked over by the bullies. They start kicking me and throwing stones at me.

I wander up the steps of the library, seeing the skeleton by the door. I open and walk in by the front desk. "Good morning," I say, "I'm afraid I'm no longer in possession of the book."

"What happened?" the dark lady asks me.

"My headmaster took it from me."

"Well, I guess I'll have to talk to your headmaster."

I brighten up, knowing that the book is not lost. She stands up and motions that I walk with her, followed by her commanding another in the library while she's gone.

I walk behind her as a duck follows a leader all the way back to the school. The clouds roll in and the wind stops as we draw closer to the school.

We arrive at the front gate, drawing attention to the dark elf I've brought to the school. I lead her to the office where the headmaster should be. "I'm looking for the headmaster," she says.

"He's busy, you'll have to wait or come back-"

"I must insist," she marches ever closer to the desk, "He's in possession of one of my books that was lent out to this student of his."

The desk woman leans over to see me cowering behind the dark woman. "Oh, *you*," she says, "Well, come on!" she stands up and motions that we follow. She knocks on the headmaster's door and opens.

"Yes?" the headmaster counts aloud as the door opens wider, "*Oh*."

"I'm aware you're in possession of one of my books, sir."

"And you are?" he retorts, setting his glasses down on the desk.

"I'm the head of the local library," she goes on, "I lent a book to one of your students, and I would like the book back-"

"I'm afraid not." The headmaster looks at me, hiding behind the librarian.

"Oh?" I can hear her becoming angry.

"That volume should be considered forbidden by the crown; it's devilish and evil!"

They stare down each other for more than a moment. The dark elf reaches out her hand, and with the other, crushes a blue jewel, whispering something arcane. Suddenly the book appears, shimmering through existence within her fingers.

"Absurd!" the headmaster shouts, trying to grab the book from her, but she moves it out of reach.

"There's nothing wrong with learning something, even if it *is* a little unconventional," she lectures, "Now that the book is within my possession, I will be leaving."

She turns to me and smiles, "You're welcome in my library *anytime.*"

Finally, after years away from home, I find myself walking the stone steps my father had put in. One by one, I arrive at the front door. *KNOCK! KNOCK!* The door opens and my mother rushes to embrace me.

"I thought you weren't coming until after graduation?" she asks.

"Headmaster barred me from attending and gave me my certificate early to kick me out of the school," I explain, she cradles my head in her chest and walks me in. "I did meet a very nice librarian who let me study after hours."

"How are you're *friends*?" she asks, holding my head straight, looking at the bruise from the bullies.

"Symphonic," I reply, shooing away her hands.

"Really? Is that good?"

"Yes." I set my case down on the ground and sit down on a chair to rest my wary feet from all the walking. "The house is exactly as we left it since last time I was home."

"Don't need to fix it if it's not broken," she responds, "I wish your father was here to celebrate with us."

I hear some cacophonic whispers, *Go outside- there's something*. I get back on my sore feet and head outside. I wander off the stone path into the garden where I find a partially skeletonized feline, the skull fully showing.

Rise, I hear; *Rise, rise, make it rise.* "*Rise,*" I say, raising my hand. Green energies flow around the animal barely clinging to life, and the body begins to twitch and it rises to its feet.

"*You,*" she pauses, "Definitely take after your father."

I kneel down and pet its mangy fur. "You could use a bath." it looks at me with empty eye sockets and lets its tongue hang down.

"Well, mother," I say, "I'm going to head back into town to look for a job."

"Take your cat with you!" she comes rushing to me to say goodbye, "She creeps me out." Lilac looks at me, smiling the best she can without a face. I pat my leg and she comes running to me, climbing all the way up to my shoulders.

"I'll be back by sundown."

I go on my walk to town, passing by the library with bones guarding the door. I go to a saloon where there's a bounty board and a man placing a paper on the cork.

"What kind of work is this?" I ask the man.

"Here," he tells me, handing me a paper, looking up to see Lilac on my shoulder, "See for yourself."

I look at the paper, written in some sort of Elvin script, I'm sure I could take it to the library. I hear chanting and shouts from the saloon, like they're celebrating something. I look around to see decorations scattered about the buildings for a local festival.

I take another look at the bounty board, full of jobs for bandits or goblins in the forest or monsters raiding farms; nothing for me to do.

The day goes on of me asking, but no opportunities for work, so I head back home. I pass by a street vendor selling small treats, so I buy one for Lilac to gnaw on on the way home. Home comes into view and she jumps down and rushes down the path.

I see mother watering the flowers as the cat rubs her head on her leg. "Any luck finding work?" She asks me.

"No, but I did find a flier," I tell her, "I'll have to get it translated."

"What's it in?" she sets the water can down and comes to greet me.

"It's in Elvin, but it's written weird."

I walk past the remains guarding the door to the library and see the head librarian sorting through books at the desk. "Good morning," I say to her, "Which aisle are the language books?"

"What kind of languages?" she responds.

"Elvin," I say. Whispers in my hear harmoniously say, *The Dwarves!* "And Dwarven, please."

"Follow me," she smiles. She stands and leads me through the maze and stops to show me the shelf. "You know I'm fluent in all major dialects on this side of the continent."

I hand her the paper the man gave me. She stares and gets a confused look on her face. "It's almost like it's written in two dialects, but it's just nonsensical."

A puzzle! they say. "I'm sure I could figure it out," I tell her as she hands it back. She goes on her way and I grab the Elvish and Dwarven dictionaries. I take the volumes and head over to my nook behind the necrotic shelf

I hold the paper up and see markings in between the lines of the Elvin in the sun, and I recognize the markings as my father's language: Dwarven. But the accents are too elegant, almost like... Elvin.

I put the paper down and start tracing the invisible markings, taking another paper and swapping accent marks, alternating the two languages. When I'm done I stare at it, listening to the thoughtful whisperings. *"Gota,"* I read from the Dwarven, meaning nothing. *Elvin! Elvin!* they say to me. I take the Elvin dictionary and scroll through the pages, looking for the word.

I find it, realizing the words are swapped, along with the accents. I work until the sun sets looking for the matching words between the two books. "Under the lions mane, you shall find me. Bring the secret and your wits. Work beneath the bridge and you will be rewarded."

"Interesting," I say to myself. I take the papers and head home for the night.

On my morning stroll with Lilac, paying close attention, I try to hit all the roads I thought might be relevant to the poem. There's no bridges nearby that relate to lions.

I come across that vendor and buy a small treat for Lilac to eat while I look around to think. "So, uh, that cat."

"Yes?" I move my attention.

"It's alive, right?" he asks.

"Yes, in a sense."

"*Okay.*"

I look around, thinking of the local state military and how their mascot is a golden lion, but I don't know of any bridges they built in the city, maybe it's another city?

"Do you know where the nearest military outpost is?" I ask the vendor. He nods and gives me directions. Lilac jumps on my shoulder and I go on my way. The sun shines at midday, but the winds are mild when I arrive.

I see the golden brass armor of the military guards standing attention. They wave to me. "I was wondering if I could ask a question?" I ask them.

"Of course!" a female guard tells me, opening her helmet, revealing eyes like ice. She seems off put by Lilac sitting on my shoulder as she looks around the new environment.

"I'm looking for a bridge that's owned by the military that's nearby?"

"The military builds a lot of bridges to ensure smooth travel over river and ravines for mass travel!" she informs me, like a saleswoman.

I recite the poem to her, and her face goes blank and we're left in a silence until the other guard bumps her shoulder and she comes back to life. "I'm sorry, I don't know what that means."

She leans over to my ear, "I'm not sure if you really want to know, but the bridge you're looking for goes over the Great Bagu River. It's a day's travel there by horse."

She starts laughing awkwardly and I start laughing as well. The other guard looks at us both and starts in on the laughing. "What was the joke?" he asks, lifting up his helmet revealing his dark skin and dark eyes.

"Oh nothin'!" she blurts out, "You should be on your way, we're on duty anyways."

"Very well," I say, turning tail, "Have a nice day."

I was able to flag down a carriage going my direction and hitch a ride to the Great Bagu River. The ride was silent, but I could hear some singing to pass the time. I watched the sun rise and almost set when we arrived.

"This is my stop!" I shout, jumping off the carriage onto the brick path.

The bridge is of white stone, with a brass lion's head on either side of the bridge. I look down to see a raging river flowing furiously beneath me.

"What might thee be looking for?" I hear someone say.

"I was looking for work, and that brought me here." I reply.

"Well, the work here depends-"

"Under the lion's mane, it says," I repeat, "Under the bridge, but I don't see any way to get down there."

"Tell me a secret and I'll I might give you what your looking for."

"My father was a dwarf-"

"Though unusual, not a secret."

"He was a necromancer," I tell him, "My mother didn't want me to know, but I figured it out. He was driven from town because of it."

"Not enough."

"In order to keep his trade secrets," I go on, "He tattooed the workings on his skin."

"And?"

"I too am a necromancer, and I will follow in his footsteps."

He falls silent and I cast my gaze from the river to this mystery man, and I find a man in brass armor clad with white fabric and brown hair.

"We could use someone of your specific skill set," he says, "I am Alastric, I'm a general in the army."

"I am-"

"I don't want your name, I'm putting together a secret research team to work under me; I only need your skills, not your name."

"Okay," I tell him, walk over to greet him. "When do I start?"

"As soon as you can," he replies.

"I can start today."

He reaches out his hand to shake, and I grab ahold. "Perfect," he smiles. He motions I follow him to his carriage, hiding behind a tree.

I see a few others resting on the carriage, and one of them waves to me. "Are you men also looking for work?"

"Aye," I hear a female voice, "I'm a woman looking for work."

"Good," I tell her, "I hope we get along."

I release the bird into the air to send a letter back home to mother. I started work in a dingy place under the earth where its dark. I find myself doing research on the dead, constantly working on animal cadavers.

"Titan!" someone calls out to me in code.

"Yes?" I reply, looking away from my work.

"I have another volume you requested."

I turn to see the person, handing me a grimoire on the dead. Forbidden volumes of magic generally censored by the crown.

I bow to thank him, and take the book to my workplace. I always find time to read these volumes. Mixing and matching the magic I find to create new, more dangerous spells.

Alastric is bringing in a new person onto the team. We walk together to the main chamber of the estate, where there's a window on the east side of the room. I find him bringing in an elf man, but his proportions are off, so perhaps he's a half elf. He's very pale with faint yellow hair.

"This is Zephrys," he announces, with the half elf waving to everybody, "He's a chemist, treat him well."

This new person goes about shaking everyone's hands. He arrives to me, "You seem different." he looks above my eyes to the symbol I've put on my forehead. "What does it mean?"

"It mean's to return to somewhere."

"I'm not too fluent in other languages, so forgive me."

I close the first grimoire of my own creation, my first volume on necrotic magic, most spells beyond my capability to cast, but it's value is apparent.

I bring the book outside of my working quarters and pass by Zephrys' working quarters, where I see a small spark, followed by a bright flash and a *HISS*. He's long gone mad, taking after my tradition and sewing the ink on his skin to keep his own secrets. He only writes his findings on himself and hoards his knowledge.

"Alastric!" I shout, walking up the steps to the main chamber.

"Yes, Titan!" he finds me, "Have you finished?"

"Yes," I reply, handing him the volume.

"You're a genius; the casters are very eager to do more with this," he takes the leather bound grimoire and kissing it.

Zephrys comes waddling out of his chamber and spins around, "I too, am close to a breakthrough!"

"Yes, I sure hope so," Alastric tells us, "You're a money pit, requesting the oddest of things."

Zephrys taps my elbow, "Let's eat, we both, *Hehe*, need a break."

We go to the eating hall and enjoy some wild turkey somebody brought in today.

Wake! Wake up! I hear shouting from my friends, only to find Zephrys in the night. "What?"

"Let's go!" he whispers.

"What do you mean?" I ask, "Where are you going?"

"I just set in motion to, uh, *collapse* this whole thing," he shakes me awake, "I've made my breakthrough! I'm leaving to the west-marches!"

"What?" I come to my senses, "You're insane!" *Go! Go with him!*

"We have to leave now! This is our chance."

"No," I say, My voices start screaming in disarray, shouting curses and spells, but they are all for not. The drown out everything around me and I see him walk out, for the last time.

And the army came in the next day and everything was dissolved. All of us were sent out, and I went back home.

I walk up these steps for the first time in a while. The sun shines and the wind blows as Lilac runs up happy as can be that I'm home. I see my mother watering the plants, wearing some new clothes. I've brought in quite the wealth with my time with Alastric, who's now deep in prison.

"Welcome home!" she rushes to hug me.

"Hey," I sink my head between her arms. The symphony has disappeared into a whirlpool of thoughts and commotion. It's too much at times.

"Hey, you okay?" she strokes my hair. Lilac rubs up against my legs.

"Yeah, I'm- I'm fine."

⇥⊙⇤

CAW! CAW! I hear a large bird making noise outside the house. My friends start imitating the bird as I stand up and open the door, only to find a falcon standing on the flowerbed. Lilac starts hissing an arches her back.

I shoo her away and close the door. I unlatch the box on the bird's back, and take out a small piece of parchment. It reads, "The west-marches is fantastic! Come and enjoy the riches it has to offer. Sincerely, Zephrys."

The bird flies off and the voices come in harmony, *Go!*

Trapped Between Two Walls

"Run!" I shout, imploring my other passengers to hurry to get to a safe stop before the airlocks fully activate.

The airlocks begin descending from the ceiling, a signal that the ship's rogue AI has infected yet another system, something that shouldn't be possible. I'm the main computer engineer, and all the systems run separately, but this AI is something beyond my skills.

I turn my head to see some people slide underneath the door before it seals shut, but someone isn't lucky enough. I turn back around and slam my head into the next airlock, falling to the ground.

Someone pulls me though before the door seals. I rush to get up to my feet, but it's too late, the next door is sealed shut. "Shit," I say.

I hear some banging on the door behind us, and the feeling of being an utter failure sets in, I should've never let the systems be 'upgraded' by our new passengers.

I pull up the radio on my chest, "Is there anyone else on this channel?"

But nothing but static talks back to me. But then, one of the alien languages we have onboard starts echoing in my radio and the intercoms scattered about. "Julk! Translate!" I command my alien comrade.

Julk listens to the repeating patterns over the radio. "It's saying to breathe your last breath."

"What?" air starts hissing from the vents, but I don't smell anything. I walk over to the wall and knock a code to the other side, saying, *I'm sorry.* Once I'm done, I walk over to my mates and bring them together in a group hug.

I start getting light-headed, and we all start dropping like flies. Finally, my eyes get dark. With my remaining senses, the room starts heating up. *BOOM!* An explosion ejects me into the vacuum of space. Where I see the entire starship bursting in two over this pit-stop of a world.

⇥⊙⇤

In Memoriam Of

Megan & Lola

Thank You

⇥◉⇤

⊷⊙⊶

Thank you again for reading.

The End.

⊷●⊶